The
Goalie's Anxiety
at the Penalty Kick

by the same author

Plays

OFFENDING THE AUDIENCE and SELF-ACCUSATION
KASPAR
THE RIDE ACROSS LAKE CONSTANCE
THEY ARE DYING OUT
MY FOOT MY TUTOR (*in* SHAKESPEARE THE SADIST
and other plays by Bauer, Fassbinder, Handke, Kroetz)

Novels

SHORT LETTER, LONG FAREWELL
A SORROW BEYOND DREAMS

The
Goalie's Anxiety
at the Penalty Kick

PETER HANDKE

translated by
Michael Roloff

EYRE METHUEN · LONDON

C. 4

First published in Great Britain in 1977
by Eyre Methuen Ltd, 11 New Fetter Lane,
London EC4P 4EE
English translation © 1972 by
Farrar, Straus and Giroux, Inc.
Originally published in German under the
title DIE ANGST DES TORMANNS BEIM ELFMETER,
© Suhrkamp Verlag, Frankfurt am Main, 1970

Printed in Great Britain by Cox & Wyman Ltd,
Fakenham, Norfolk

ISBN 0 413 45080 5

BL JAN 2 8 '80

"The goalie watched as the ball rolled across the line . . ."

When Joseph Bloch, a building worker who had once been a well-known goalkeeper, reported for work that morning, he was told that he was fired. At least that was how he interpreted the fact that no one except the foreman looked up from his tea-break when he appeared at the door of the site hut, where the workers happened to be at that moment, and Bloch left the building site. Out on the street he raised his arm, but the car that drove past – even though Bloch hadn't been hailing a taxi – was not a taxi. Then he heard the sound of brakes in front of him. Bloch turned round: behind him there was a taxi; its driver started swearing. Bloch turned round again, got in, and told the driver to take him to the Naschmarkt.

It was a beautiful October day. Bloch ate a sausage at a stand and then walked through the market to a cinema. Everything he saw disturbed him. He tried to notice as little as possible. Inside the cinema he breathed freely.

Afterwards he was astonished by the perfectly natural way the girl at the cash desk had responded to the wordless gesture with which he'd put his money on the box-office turntable. Next to the screen he noticed the illuminated dial of an electric clock. Halfway through the film he heard a bell; for a long time he couldn't decide whether the chiming was in the film or coming from the church tower outside near the Naschmarkt.

Out on the street, he bought some grapes, which were especially cheap at this time of year. He walked on, eating the grapes and spitting out the skins. The first hotel where he asked for a room turned him away because he had only a briefcase with him; the receptionist at the second hotel, which was on a side street, took him to his room himself. Even before the man had gone, Bloch lay down on the bed and was soon asleep.

In the evening he left the hotel and got drunk. Later he sobered up and tried ringing some friends; since most of these friends didn't live in the city and the phone didn't return his coins, Bloch soon ran out of change. A policeman to whom Bloch shouted, thinking he could get his attention, did not respond. Bloch wondered whether the policeman might have misconstrued the words Bloch had called across the street, and he remembered the natural way the cinema cashier had spun around the tray with his ticket. He'd been so astonished by the swiftness of her movements that he almost forgot to pick up the ticket. He decided to look up the cashier.

When he got back to the cinema, the lights were just going out. Bloch saw a man on a ladder changing the letters of the film for tomorrow's title. He waited until he could read the name of the next film; then he went back to the hotel.

The next day was Saturday. Bloch decided to stay at the hotel one more day. Except for an American couple, he was alone in the dining room; for a while he listened to their conversation, which he could understand fairly well because he'd travelled with his team to several matches in New York; then he quickly went out to buy some newspapers. Because they were the weekend editions, the papers were very heavy; he didn't fold them up but carried them under his arm to the hotel. He sat down at his table, which had been cleared in the meantime, and took out the classified section; this depressed him. Outside he saw two people walking by with thick newspapers. He held his breath until they had passed. Only then did he realize they were the two Americans. Having seen them earlier only at the table in the dining room, he did not recognise them.

At a cafe he took a long time drinking the glass of water

served with his coffee. Once in a while he got up and took a magazine from the piles lying on the chairs and tables set aside for them; once, when the waitress retrieved the magazines piled beside him, she muttered the phrase "newspaper table" as she left. Bloch, who could hardly bear looking at the magazines but at the same time could not really put down a single one of them before he had leafed through it completely, tried glancing out at the street now and then; the contrast between the magazine illustrations and the changing views outside soothed him. As he left, he returned the magazines to the table himself.

At the market the stalls were already closed. For a few minutes Bloch casually kicked discarded vegetables and fruit along the ground in front of him. Somewhere between the stalls he relieved himself. Standing there, he noticed that the walls of the wooden stands were black with urine everywhere.

The grape skins he had spat out the day before were still lying on the pavement. When Bloch put his money on the cashier's tray, the note got caught as the turntable revolved; he had a chance to say something. The cashier answered. He said something else. Because this was unusual, the girl looked up. This gave him an excuse to go on talking. Inside the cinema, Bloch remembered the cheap novel and the hot-plate next to the cashier; he leaned back and began to take in the details on the screen.

Late in the afternoon he took a tram to the stadium. He bought standing room but sat down on the newspapers, which he still hadn't thrown away; the fact that the spectators in front of him blocked his view did not bother him. During the game most of them sat down. Bloch wasn't recognized. He left the newspapers where they were, put a beer bottle on top of them, and went out of the stadium before the final whistle, so that he wouldn't get caught in the rush. The large number of almost empty buses and trams waiting outside the stadium – it was a league match – seemed strange. He sat down in a tram. He sat there almost alone for so long that he began to feel impatient. Had the referee called extra? When Bloch looked up, he saw that the sun was going down. Without meaning anything by it, Bloch lowered his head.

Outside, it suddenly got windy. At just about the time that the final whistle blew, three long separate blasts, the drivers and conductors got into the buses and trams and the people crowded out of the stadium. Bloch could imagine the noise of beer bottles landing on the playing field; at the same time he could hear the dust hitting against the windows. Just as he had leaned back in the cinema, so now, while the match-goers surged into the tram, he leaned forward. Luckily, he still had a programme from the cinema. It felt as though the floodlights had just been turned on in the stadium. "Nonsense," Bloch said to himself. He never played well under the lights.

In the city centre he spent some time trying to find a phone box; when he found an empty one, the receiver was lying on the floor, the wires torn out of their socket. He walked on. Finally he was able to make a call from the West Railway Station. Since it was Saturday, hardly anybody was at home. When a woman he used to know finally answered, he had to talk a bit before she realized who he was. They arranged to meet at a restaurant near the station, where Bloch knew there was a juke box. He passed the time until she came by putting coins in the juke box, letting other people choose the songs; meanwhile, he looked at the signed photos of football players on the walls. The place had been leased a couple of years ago by a forward who played for Austria and who'd then gone overseas as coach of one of the unofficial American sides; now that the league had broken up, he'd disappeared over there. Bloch started talking to a girl at the table next to the juke box, who kept choosing the same record by reaching behind her without looking at the machine. She left with him. He tried to get her into an entrance way, but all the outside doors were already locked. When they did get one open, it turned out that, to judge from the singing, a religious service was going on behind an inner door. They found a lift; Bloch pushed the button for the top floor. Even before the lift started, the girl wanted to get out again. Bloch then pushed the button for the second floor; they got out there and stood on the stairs; now the girl became affectionate. They ran upstairs together. The lift was on the top floor; they got in, rode down and went back out on to the street.

Bloch walked beside the girl for a while; then he turned around and went back to the restaurant. The woman whom Bloch had rung was waiting. She still had her coat on. Bloch explained to the first girl's girlfriend, who was still at the table next to the juke box, that her friend would not come back, and went out of the restaurant with the woman.

Bloch said, "I feel silly without a coat when you're wearing one." The woman took his arm. To free his arm, Bloch pretended that he wanted to show her something. Then he didn't know what it was he wanted to show her. Suddenly he felt the urge to buy an evening paper. They walked through several streets but couldn't find a news-stand. Finally they took the bus to the South Station, but it was already closed. Bloch pretended to be startled; and in reality he was startled. To the woman – who had hinted, by opening her handbag on the bus and fiddling with various things, that she was having her period – he said, "I forgot to leave a note," without knowing what he actually meant by the words "note" and "leave". Anyway, he got into a cab alone and drove to the Naschmarkt.

Since the cinema had a late show on Saturdays, Bloch actually arrived too early. He went to a nearby snack bar, and, standing up, ate a sausage. He tried to tell the counter girl a joke as fast as he could; when the time was up and he still hadn't finished, he stopped in the middle of a sentence and paid. The girl laughed.

On the street he ran into a man he knew who asked him for money. Bloch swore at him. As the drunk grabbed Bloch by the shirt, the street went dark. Startled, the drunk let go. Bloch, who now realised that the cinema lights would be going out, rushed away. In front of the cinema he met the cashier;

she was getting into a car with a man. Bloch watched her. When she was in the car, in the seat next to the driver, she answered his look by tucking her dress under her; at least Bloch took this to be a response. There were no incidents; she had closed the door and the car had driven off.

Bloch went back to the hotel. He found the lobby lit up but deserted. When he took his key from the hook, a folded note fell out of the pigeonhole. He opened it: it was his bill. While Bloch stood there in the lobby, with the note in his hand gazing at the single suitcase that stood near the door, the receptionist came out of the boxroom. Bloch immediately asked him for a newspaper and at the same time looked through the open door into the boxroom, where the man had evidently been dozing on a chair he'd taken from the lobby. The receptionist closed the door, so that all Bloch could see was a small stepladder with a soup bowl on top of it, and said nothing until he was behind the desk. But Bloch had understood even the closing of the door as a rebuff and walked upstairs to his room. In the rather long hall he noticed a pair of shoes in front of only one door; in his room he took off his own shoes without untying them and put them outside the door. He lay down on the bed and fell asleep at once.

In the middle of the night he was briefly awakened by a quarrel in the adjoining room; but perhaps his ears were so oversensitive after suddenly waking up that he only thought the voices next door were quarrelling. He slammed his fist against the wall. Then he heard a tap being turned on. The water was turned off; it became quiet, and he fell back to sleep.

Next morning Bloch was woken up by the telephone. He was asked whether he wanted to stay another night. Looking at his briefcase on the floor – the room had no luggage rack – Bloch immediately said yes and hung up. After he had brought in his shoes, which had not been cleaned, probably because it was Sunday, he left the hotel without breakfast.

In the wash-room at the South Station he gave himself a

shave with an electric razor. He took a shower in one of the shower cubicles. While getting dressed, he read the sports section and the court reports in the newspaper. Afterwards – he was still reading and it was rather quiet in the adjoining booths – he suddenly felt good. Fully dressed, he leaned against the wall of the booth and kicked his foot against the wooden bench. The noise brought a question from the attendant outside and, when Bloch didn't answer, a knock on the door. When he still didn't reply, the woman outside slapped a towel (or whatever it might be) against the door handle and went away. Bloch finished reading the paper standing up.

On the square in front of the station he ran into a man he knew who told him he was going out to the suburbs to referee a minor-league match. Bloch thought this was a joke and played along with it by saying that he might as well come too, as linesman. When his friend opened his duffle-bag and showed him the referee's uniform and a net bag full of lemons, Bloch saw even these things, in line with the initial idea, as some kind of trick items from a novelty shop and, still playing along, said that, since he was coming too, he might as well carry the duffel-bag. Later, when he was with his friend on the suburban train, the duffel-bag in his lap, it seemed, especially since it was lunchtime and the compartment was nearly empty, as though he was going through this whole business only as a joke. Though what the empty compartment was supposed to have to do with his frivolous behaviour was not clear to Bloch. That this friend of his was going to the suburbs with a duffel-bag; that he, Bloch, was coming along; that they had lunch together at a local pub and went together to what Bloch called "an honest-to-goodness football pitch", all this seemed to him, even while he was travelling back home alone – he had not liked the game – some kind of mutual pretence. None of that mattered, thought Bloch. Luckily, he didn't run into anyone else on the square in front of the station.

From a phone box at the edge of a park he called his ex-wife; she said everything was fine but didn't ask about him. Bloch felt uneasy.

He sat down in a garden cafe that was still open despite the season and ordered a beer. When, after some time, nobody had brought his beer, he left; besides, the steel tabletop, which wasn't covered by a cloth, had been blinding him. He stood outside the window of a restaurant; the people inside were sitting in front of a television. He watched for a while. Somebody turned towards him, and he walked away.

In the Prater he was mugged. One thug jerked his jacket over his arms from behind; the other butted his head against Bloch's chin. Bloch's knees folded a little, then he gave the thug in front a kick. Finally the two of them shoved him behind a sweet stall and finished the job. He fell down and they left. Bloch cleaned off his face and suit in a public convenience.

At a cafe near the Prater he played billiards until it was time for the sports news on television. Bloch asked the waitress to turn on the set and then watched as if none of it had anything to do with him. He asked the waitress to join him for a drink. When the waitress came out of the back room, where gambling was going on, Bloch was already at the door; she walked past him but didn't speak. Bloch went out.

Back at the Naschmarkt, the sight of the sloppily piled fruit and vegetable crates behind the stalls seemed like another joke of some kind, something not quite serious. Like cartoons without captions, thought Bloch, who liked cartoons without captions. This feeling of pretence, of playing around – "This business with the referee's whistle in the duffel-bag," thought Bloch – only went away when he was in the cinema and the comic picked up a trumpet from a junk shop as if by accident and started tooting on it as though it were the most natural thing in the world; then Bloch realised that this trumpet and all other objects as well were straightforward and unambiguous. Bloch relaxed.

After the film he waited between the market stalls for the cashier. Some time after the start of the last show, she came out. So. as not to frighten her by coming at her from between the stalls, he sat there on a crate until she got to the more brightly lit part of the Naschmarkt. Behind the lowered shutter in one of the stalls, a telephone was ringing; the stand's phone number was written in large numerals on the corrugated iron. "Not available," Bloch thought at once. He followed the cashier without actually catching up with her. As she got on the bus, he strolled up and stepped aboard after her. He took a seat facing her but left several rows of seats between them. Not until new passengers blocked his view at the next stop was Bloch able to think again. She had certainly looked at him but obviously hadn't recognized him; had the mugging changed his looks that much? Bloch ran his fingers over his face. The idea of glancing at the window to check what she was doing struck him as foolish. He pulled the newspaper from the inside pocket of his jacket and looked down at the letters but didn't read. Then, suddenly, he found himself reading. An eyewitness was testifying about the murder of a pimp who'd been shot in the eye at close range. "A bat flew out of the back of his head and slammed against the wallpaper. My heart skipped a beat." When, without a new paragraph, the sentences went straight on to something else, to an entirely different person, Bloch was startled. "But they should have put a paragraph there," thought Bloch. After his abrupt shock, he was furious. He walked down the gangway toward the cashier and sat diagonally opposite her, so that he could look at her; but he did not look at her.

When they got off the bus, Bloch realized that they were far outside the city, near the airport. At this time of night, it was a very quiet area. Bloch walked along beside the girl but not as if he were escorting her or even as if he wanted to. After a while he touched her. The girl stopped, turned, and touched him too, so fiercely that he was startled. For a moment the handbag in her other hand seemed more familiar to him than she did.

They walked along together a while, but keeping their

distance, not touching. Only when they were on the stairs did he touch her again. She started to run; he walked more slowly. When he got upstairs, he knew which was her flat by the wide-open door. In the darkness she let him know where she was; he went over to her and they went in together straight away.

In the morning, woken by a noise, he looked out of the window and saw a plane coming in to land. The blinking of the navigation lights on the machine made him close the curtains. Because they hadn't turned on any lights, the curtains had stayed open. Bloch lay down and closed his eyes.

With his eyes closed, he was overcome by a strange inability to visualize anything. He tried to tell himself the names he knew for each thing in the room, but he couldn't picture anything; not even the plane he had just seen landing, though he might have been able to recall to mind, probably from earlier experience, the screech its brakes were making now on the runway. He opened his eyes and looked for a while at the corner where the kitchen was: he concentrated on the kettle and the wilted flowers drooping in the sink. Hardly had he closed his eyes again, but he could no longer imagine the flowers and the kettle. He resorted to thinking up sentences about the things instead of words for them, in the belief that a story made up of such sentences would help him remember what the things looked like. The kettle whistled. The flowers had been given to the girl by a friend. Nobody took the kettle off the hot plate. "Would you like some tea?" asked the girl. It was no use: Bloch opened his eyes when he couldn't stand it any more. The girl beside him was asleep.

Bloch grew nervous. If the pressure of his surroundings was bad when his eyes were open, the pressure of the words for the objects surrounding him was even worse when his eyes were closed. "Maybe it's because I've just slept with her," he thought. He went into the bathroom and took a long shower.

The kettle really was whistling when he came back. "The shower woke me up," the girl said. Bloch felt as if she were talking to him directly for the first time. He wasn't quite

16

himself yet, he replied. Were there ants in the teapot? "Ants?" When the boiling water from the kettle hit the bottom of the pot, instead of tea leaves he saw the ants which he had once doused with scalding water. He pulled the curtains open again.

The tea in the open canister seemed – since the light reached it only through the small round hole for the lid – oddly illuminated by the reflection from the inner walls. Bloch, sitting with the canister at the table, was staring fixedly through the hole. It amused him to be so fascinated by the peculiar glow of the tea leaves while inattentively talking to the girl. Finally he pressed the lid back on the top, but at the same time stopped talking. The girl hadn't noticed anything. "My name is Gerda," she said. Bloch hadn't even wanted to know. He asked whether she had noticed anything, but she'd put on a record, an Italian song with electric-guitar accompaniment. "I like his voice," she said. Bloch who had no use for Italian pop songs, remained silent.

When she went out briefly to get something for breakfast – "It's Monday," she said – Bloch finally had a chance to study everything carefully. During breakfast they talked a lot. After a time Bloch noticed that she talked about things he'd just told her as if they were her own, but when he mentioned something she had just talked about, he either quoted her exactly or, if he was using his own words, always started with a hesitant "this" or "that", as if he were afraid of making her affairs his and wanted to keep them at a distance. If he talked about the foreman, say, or about a football player named Stumm, she could say, almost at once, quite familiarly, "the foreman" and "Stumm"; however, when she mentioned someone she knew called Freddy or a bar called Stephanskeller, he invariably talked about "this Freddy?" and "that Stephans Keller?" when he replied. Everything she mentioned deterred him from taking any deeper interest, and it upset him that she seemed so free to take over whatever he said.

From time to time, of course, the conversation became as

17

natural for him as for her; he asked a question and she answered; she asked one and he made the obvious reply. "Is that a jet?" – "No, it's got propellers." – "Where do you live?" – "Near the Prater." He even came close to telling her about the mugging.

But then everything began to irritate him more and more. He wanted to answer her but broke off in mid-sentence because he assumed that she already knew what he was going to say. She grew restless and started moving about the room; she was looking for something to do, occasionally smiling rather pointlessly. Changing the records and playing the other side passed a certain amount of time. She got up and lay down on the bed; he sat down next to her. Was he going to work today? she wanted to know.

Suddenly he was strangling her. From the start his grip was so tight that she never had a chance to think he was kidding. Bloch heard voices outside in the hall. He was scared to death. He noticed some stuff running out of her nose. She was gurgling. Finally he heard a snapping noise. It sounded like a stone on an unmade road slamming against the bottom of a car. Saliva had dripped onto the linoleum.

The sense of panic had been so fierce that all at once he was exhausted. He lay down on the floor, unable to fall asleep but incapable of raising his head. He heard someone slap a duster against the outside doorknob. He listened. There had been nothing to hear. So he must have fallen asleep after all.

It didn't take him long to wake up; as soon as his eyes were open, he felt exposed; as though there was a draught in the room, he thought. And he hadn't even scraped his skin. Still, he imagined that some kind of lymph fluid was seeping out through all his pores. He was up and had wiped off everything in the room with a dish cloth.

He looked out of the window: down below, somebody with an armful of coats on hangers was running across the grass toward a delivery van.

He left by the lift and walked for a while without changing

18

direction. Then he took a local bus to the tram terminus; from there he rode back to the city centre.

When he got to the hotel, it turned out that his briefcase had already been brought downstairs for safekeeping, since it looked as if he wouldn't be back. While he was paying his bill, the porter fetched the briefcase from the boxroom. Bloch saw a faint ring on it and realized that a wet milk bottle must have been standing on it; he opened the case while the receptionist was getting his change and noticed that the contents had been inspected: the toothbrush handle was sticking out of its leather case; the portable radio was lying on top. Bloch turned towards the porter, but he had disappeared into the boxroom. The space behind the desk was quite narrow, so Bloch was able to pull the receptionist towards him with one hand and then, after a sharp breath, to feint punching his face with the other. The man flinched, though Bloch had not even touched him. The porter in the boxroom kept quiet. Bloch had already left with his briefcase.

He got to the company's personnel officer at exactly the right time, just before lunch, and picked up his papers. Bloch was surprised that they weren't there ready for him and that some phone calls still had to be made. He asked to use the phone himself and called his ex-wife; when the child answered the phone and immediately launched parrot-fashion into a message about his mother not being home, Bloch hung up. The papers were ready by now; he put the income-tax form in his briefcase. Before he could ask the woman about his back pay, she was gone. Bloch counted out the money for the phone call onto the table and left the building.

The banks were also closed for lunch by now. Bloch hung around in a park until he could withdraw the money from his current account – he'd never had a savings account. Since that wouldn't take him very far, he decided to return the transistor radio, which was practically brand-new. He took the bus to his place near the Prater and fetched his flash attachment and electric razor as well. At the shop they explained that the

19

goods couldn't be returned, only exchanged. Bloch took the bus back to his room and came away with a suitcase containing two trophies – of course, they were only copies of cups his team had won, one in a tournament and the other in a championship game – and a gold-plated pendant in the shape of two football boots.

In the junk shop no one came for a time so he took out his things and simply put them on the counter. Then he felt that he'd put the things on the counter too confidently, as though he'd already sold them, and he whisked them back off the counter and hid them in his bag; he would put them back on the counter only after he'd been asked to. On the back of a shelf he noticed a china music box with a dancer striking the familiar pose. As usual when he saw a music box, he felt that he'd seen it before. Without haggling, he simply accepted the first offer for his things.

With the lightweight coat he had taken from his room across his arm, he had then gone to the South Station. On his way to the bus stop, he had run into the woman at whose news-stand he usually bought his paper. She was wearing a fur coat and was out walking her dog. Even though he usually said something to her when he bought a paper, looking at her blackened fingertips and handing over his money, here, away from her stand, she seemed not to know him; at least she didn't look up and hadn't answered his greeting.

Since there were only a few trains to the border each day, Bloch spent the time until the next train sleeping in the news cinema. At one point it got very bright and the sound of a curtain opening or closing seemed ominously close. To see whether the curtain had opened or closed, Bloch opened his eyes. Somebody was shining a torch in his face. Bloch knocked the light out of the usher's hand and went into the men's toilets.

It was quiet here; daylight was filtering in. Bloch stood still for a while.

The usher had followed him and threatened to call the

police. Bloch had turned on the tap, washed his hands, then pushed the button on the electric dryer and held his hands under the warm air until the usher disappeared.

Then Bloch had cleaned his teeth. He had watched in the mirror how he rubbed one hand across his teeth while the other, loosely clenched into a fist, rested oddly against his chest. From inside the cinema he heard the shouting and roaring of the cartoon figures.

Bloch remembered that an ex-girlfriend of his ran a pub in a place near the border in the south. In the station post office, where they had phone books for the entire country, he couldn't find her number; there were several pubs in the village, and their owners weren't listed; besides, lifting the phone books – they were all hanging in a row, spine upwards – soon proved too much for him. "Face down," he thought suddenly. A policeman came in and asked for his papers.

Looking down at the passport and then up at Bloch's face, the policeman said that the usher had lodged a complaint. After a while Bloch decided to apologize. But the policeman had already returned the passport, with the comment that Bloch certainly got around a bit. Bloch didn't watch him go but quickly tipped the phone book back into place. Somebody was shouting; when Bloch looked up, he saw a Greek work-man talking loudly into the phone in the booth right in front of him. Bloch thought things over and decided to take the bus instead of the train; he exchanged his ticket and, after buying a salami sandwich and several newspapers, finally went out to the bus station.

The bus was already there, though of course the door was still closed; the drivers stood talking in a group not far away. Bloch sat on a bench; the sun was shining. He ate the salami sandwich but left the papers lying next to him, because he wanted to save them for the long ride.

The luggage boots on either side of the bus remained quite empty; there was hardly anybody with luggage. Bloch waited outside until the folding door at the back was closed. Then he quickly got in at the front, and the bus started. There was a shout from outside and it stopped again immediately. Bloch did not turn around; a farm woman got on with a child who was crying noisily. Inside, the child quietened down; then the bus moved off.

Bloch noticed that he was sitting on a seat right over a wheel; his feet slipped down off the curve the floor made at that point. He moved to the seats right at the back, where, if necessary, he could easily look behind. As he sat down, his eyes met the driver's in the rearview mirror, but there was nothing significant about it. The movement Bloch made to stow away the briefcase behind him gave him a chance to look outside. The folding door was rattling noisily.

While the other seats all faced the front of the bus, the two rows directly in front of him faced each other; therefore, most of the passengers seated behind one another stopped talking almost as soon as the bus started, but those in front of him started talking again almost immediately. Bloch found the sound of their voices quite pleasant; it was relaxing to be able to listen.

After a while – the bus was now on the main road – a woman sitting next to him pointed out that he had dropped some change. "Is that your money?" she asked as she fished a single coin out from between the seat and the backrest. Another coin, an American cent, lay on the seat between them. Bloch took the coins, explaining that he'd probably lost them when he'd turned around. But since the woman had not noticed that he had turned around, she began to ask questions and Bloch went on answering; gradually, although the way they were sitting made it uncomfortable, they began to talk to each other a little.

Between talking and listening, Bloch did not put the coins away. They had become warm in his hand, as if they had just come from a cinema box office. The coins were so dirty, he said, because they had been used recently at a football match to decide the toss. "I don't understand things like football,"

22

the woman said. Bloch hastily opened his newspaper. "Heads or tails," she went on, so that Bloch had to fold the paper up again. Earlier, when he had been in the seat over the wheel, the loop inside his overcoat, which he had hung up on the hook just above him, had been torn off when he had sat down sharply on the part of the coat which was dangling on the seat. With his coat on his knees, Block was defenceless sitting next to the woman.

The road was bumpier now. Because the rear door did not fit properly, Bloch noticed how the light from outside flickered into the bus intermittently through the slit. Without looking at the slit, he was aware of the light flickering over his paper. He read line by line. Then he looked up and watched the passengers at the front of the bus. The farther away they sat, the nicer it was to look at them. After a while he noticed that the flickering had stopped. Outside, it had grown dark.

Bloch, who was not used to noticing so many details, had a headache, perhaps also because of the smell from all the newspapers he had with him. Luckily, the bus stopped in a market town, where a restaurant was serving a late meal for passengers. While Bloch was walking about outside for a bit, he could hear the cigarette machine in the bar being operated again and again.

He noticed a lighted phone box in front of the restaurant. His ears were still humming from the drone of the bus, so he was glad of the crunch of gravel by the phone box. He tossed the newspapers into a litter bin next to the phone box and closed the door behind him. "I make a good target." Once in a movie he had heard somebody say that standing by a window at night.

Nobody answered. Outside again in the shadow of the phone box, Bloch could hear the loud pinging of the pinball machines through the drawn curtains of the bar. When he went in, it turned out to be almost empty; most of the passengers had already gone outside. Bloch drank a beer standing up and went out into the hall: some people were already in the bus, others stood by the door talking to the driver, and more stood farther away in the dark with their backs to the bus. Bloch, who was getting sick of such observations, wiped his hand across his mouth. Why didn't he just look away? He looked away and saw some passengers in the hall coming back from the lavatory with their children. When he had wiped his mouth, his hand had smelled of the metal handrails on the back of the seats. "That can't be true," Bloch thought. The driver had got into the bus and, to signal that everybody else should get in too, had started the engine. "As if we didn't know what he wanted without that," Bloch thought. As they drove off, the road was showered with sparks from the cigarettes thrown hastily from the window.

Nobody was sitting next to him now. Bloch retreated into the corner and put his legs up on the seat. He untied his shoes, leaned against the side window, and looked over at the window on the other side. He held his hands behind his neck, pushed a crumb off the seat with his foot, pressed his arms against his ears, and looked at his elbows in front of him. He pushed the insides of his elbows against his temples, sniffed at his shirtsleeves, rubbed his chin against his upper arm, laid back his head, and looked up at the lights in the roof. There was no end to it any more. The only thing he could think of was to sit up.

The shadows of the trees standing on the far side of the ditches seemed to circle around the trees themselves as the bus went by. The windscreen wipers did not point in exactly the same direction. The ticket tray next to the driver seemed open. Something that may have been a glove lay in the gangway. Cows were sleeping in the meadows next to the road. There was no point in denying that.

Gradually more and more passengers got off at their stops. They stood next to the driver until he let them out at the front. When the bus was not moving, Bloch heard the canvas flapping on the roof. Then the bus stopped again, and he heard welcoming shouts outside in the dark. Further on, he recognized a level crossing without gates.

Just before midnight the bus stopped at the border village. Bloch immediately took a room at the small hotel right by the bus stop. He asked the girl who showed him upstairs about his girlfriend, whose first name – Hertha – was all he knew. She was able to tell him that his girlfriend had leased a pub just outside the village. In the room Bloch asked the girl, who was still in the doorway, what that noise was all about. "They're still playing skittles," the girl answered and left. Without looking around, Bloch undressed, washed his hands, and lay down on the bed. The rumbling and crashing downstairs went on for quite a while. But Bloch had already fallen asleep.

He did not wake up by himself but must have been roused by something. Everything was quiet. Bloch thought about what might have wakened him; after a while he began to imagine that the sound of a newspaper opening had startled him. Or had it been the creaking of the wardrobe? Maybe a coin had fallen out of his trousers, hung carelessly over the chair, and had rolled under the bed. On the wall he noticed an engraving that showed the town at the time of the Turkish wars; the townspeople strolled outside the walls; in the bell-tower behind the walls the bell was hanging at such an angle that you had to suppose that it was ringing loudly. Bloch thought about the sexton being lifted up bodily by the bell rope. He noticed that all the townspeople were walking toward the gate in the wall; one child apparently was stumbling because of a dog slinking between his legs. Even the little auxiliary chapel bell was pictured in such a way that it almost tipped over. Under the bed there had only been a used match. From out in the corridor, farther away, there came again the sound of a key in a lock; that must have been what had roused him.

At breakfast Bloch heard that a schoolboy with a spinal defect had been missing for two days. The girl talked about this to the bus driver, who had spent the night at the hotel before driving back in what Bloch could see from the window

25

was an almost empty bus. Later the girl left too, so that Bloch was left sitting in the dining room by himself for a while. He put a pile of newspapers on the chair next to him; he read that it was not a cripple but a boy with a *speech* defect that was missing. Above him, a hoover was going – as the girl explained on her return, as though she ought to account for it. Bloch didn't know what to say to that. Then empty beer bottles clinked in the crates being carried across the yard outside. The voices of the delivery men in the hall sounded to Bloch as though they came from the television set next door. The girl had told him that the innkeeper's mother sat in that room watching the daytime programmes.

Later on Bloch bought himself a shirt, some underwear, and several pairs of socks in a general store. The shop girl, who had taken her time coming out of the rather dim storage room, seemed not to understand Bloch, who was speaking to her in complete sentences; only when he recited one by one the words for the things he wanted did she begin to move again. As she opened the cash-register drawer, she had said that some rubber boots had also just arrived; and as she was handing him his things in a plastic carrier bag, she had asked whether he needed anything else: handkerchiefs? a tie? a pull-over? At the hotel Bloch had changed and stuffed his dirty clothes in the plastic bag. He met hardly anyone outside in the square or on his way out of the village. At a building site a cement mixer was just being turned off; it was so quiet now that his own steps sounded almost indecent to Bloch. He had stopped and looked at the tarpaulins covering the timber stacks outside a sawmill as if there were something else to hear besides the murmur of the sawmill workers' voices from behind the timber stacks where they were probably taking their tea-break.

He had found out that the pub, along with a couple of farmhouses and the customs post, stood at a spot where the made-up road curved back towards the village; branching off from the road was a track, which was likewise made up near the

26

houses, but further on was only covered with gravel, and then, just before the border, turned into a footpath. The border crossing was closed. Actually Bloch had not even asked about the border crossing.

He saw a hawk circling over a field. When the hawk hovered at one spot and then dived down, Bloch realized that he had not been watching the hawk fluttering and diving but the spot in the field for which the bird would presumably head; the hawk had checked itself in its dive and soared up again.

It was also odd that, while he was walking past a field of maize, Bloch did not look straight down the rows that ran through to the end of the field but saw only an impenetrable thicket of stalks, leaves, and corncobs, with here and there some naked kernels showing as well. As well? The brook which the road crossed at that point was rushing by quite noisily, and Bloch stopped.

At the pub he found a barmaid just scrubbing the floor. Bloch asked for the landlady. "She's still asleep," the barmaid said. Without sitting down, Bloch ordered a beer. The barmaid lifted a chair off the table. Bloch took the second chair off the table and sat down.

The barmaid went behind the bar. Bloch put his hands on the table. The barmaid bent down and opened the bottle. Bloch pushed the ashtray aside. The barmaid took a beer-mat from another table as she passed it. Bloch pushed his chair back. The barmaid took the glass, which had been slipped over the neck of the bottle, off the bottle, set the beer-mat on the table, put the glass on the mat, tipped the bottle into the glass, put the bottle on the table, and went away. It was starting up again. Bloch did not know what to do any more.

Finally he noticed a drop running down the outside of the glass and, on the wall, a clock whose hands were two matches; one match was broken off and served as the hour hand. He had not watched the descending drop but the spot on the beer-mat that the drop might hit. The barmaid, who was meanwhile waxing the floor, asked if he knew the landlady. Bloch

27

nodded, but only when the barmaid looked up did he say yes.

A little girl ran in without closing the door. The barmaid sent her back to wipe her boots and, after a second reminder, to shut the door. "The landlady's kid," explained the barmaid, who took the child straight into the kitchen. When she came back, she said that a few days ago a man had wanted to see the landlady. "He claimed that he had been sent to dig a well. She wanted to send him away immediately, but he wouldn't let up until she showed him the cellar, and as soon as he was down there he grabbed a spade, so that she had to fetch help to get him to leave, and she . . ." Bloch barely managed to interrupt her. "The kid has been scared ever since that the well-digger might turn up again." But in the meantime a customs guard came in and had a drink at the bar.

Was the missing schoolboy back home again? the barmaid asked. The customs guard answered, "No, he hasn't been found yet."

"Well, he hasn't been gone for even two days yet," the barmaid said. The guard replied, "But the nights are beginning to get quite chilly now."

"Anyway, he's warmly dressed," said the barmaid. The guard agreed that, yes, he was dressed warmly.

"He can't be far," he added. He couldn't have got very far, the barmaid repeated. Bloch noticed a damaged set of antlers over the juke box. The barmaid explained that it came from a stag that had wandered into the minefield.

From the kitchen he heard sounds that, as he listened, turned into voices. The barmaid was shouting through the closed door. The landlady was answering from the kitchen. They talked to each other like that a while. Then, halfway through an answer, the landlady came in. Bloch said hello.

She sat down at his table, not next to but across from him; she put her hands on her knees under the table. Through the open door Bloch could hear the hum of the refrigerator in the kitchen. The child sat next to it, eating a sandwich. The landlady looked at him as if it was too long since she had last seen him. "I haven't seen you for a long time," she said. Bloch told her a story about his visit here. Through the door, quite far away, he saw the little girl sitting in the kitchen. The landlady put her hands on the table and turned the palms over and back. The barmaid brought the drink Bloch had ordered for her. Which "her"? In the kitchen, which was now empty, the refrigerator rattled. Through the door Bloch looked at the apple parings lying on the kitchen table. Under the table there was a bowl heaped full of apples; a few apples had rolled off and were scattered around on the floor. A pair of overalls hung on a nail in the doorframe. The landlady had pushed the ashtray between herself and Bloch. Bloch put the bottle to one side, but she put the match-box in front of her and set the glass down next to it. Finally Bloch pushed his glass and the bottle to the right of them. Hertha laughed.

The little girl had come back and was leaning against the back of the landlady's chair. She was sent to get wood for the kitchen, but when she opened the door with only one hand, she dropped the logs. The barmaid picked up the wood and carried it into the kitchen while the child went back to leaning against the back of the landlady's chair. It seemed to Bloch as if these proceedings could be used against him.

Somebody tapped on the window from outside but disappeared immediately. The estate owner's son, the landlady said. Then some children walked by outside, and one of them darted up and pressed his face against the glass and ran away again. "School's over," she said. Suddenly it got darker inside because a furniture van had pulled up outside. "There's my furniture," said the landlady. Bloch was relieved that he could get up and help bring in the furniture.

As they were carrying the wardrobe, one of its doors swung open. Bloch kicked the door shut again. When the wardrobe was set down in the bedroom, the door opened again. One of the vanmen handed Bloch the key, and Bloch turned it in the lock. But he wasn't the owner, Bloch said. Gradually, when he said something now, he himself reappeared in what he said.

29

The landlady asked him to stay for lunch. Bloch, who had planned to stay at her place anyway, refused. But he'd come back this evening. Hertha, who was talking from the room with the furniture, answered as he was going out; at least, it seemed to him that he had heard her call out something. He stepped back into the bar, but all he could see through the doors standing open everywhere was the barmaid at the stove in the kitchen while the landlady was putting clothes into the wardrobe in the bedroom and the child was doing her home-work at a table in the bar. He had probably confused the water boiling over on the stove with a shout.

Even though the window was open, it was impossible to see into the customs shed; the room was too dark from the outside. Still, somebody must have seen Bloch from the inside; he noticed that he himself was holding his breath as he walked past. Was it possible that nobody was in the room even though the window was wide open? Why "even though"? Was it possible that nobody was in the room because the window was wide open? Bloch looked back: a beer bottle had even been taken off the windowsill so that they could have a better look at him. He heard a sound like a bottle rolling under a sofa. On the other hand, it was not likely that the customs shed had a sofa. Only when he had gone further on did it become clear to him that a radio had been turned on in the room. Bloch went back along the wide curve the road made towards the town. At one point he started to run with relief because of the openness and simplicity with which the road led back to the village.

He wandered among the houses for a while. At a cafe he chose a few records after the owner had turned on the juke box; he had walked out even before all the records had played. Outside, he heard the owner unplug the machine. On the benches sat the schoolchildren waiting for the bus.

He stopped in front of a fruit stall but stood so far away from it that the woman behind the stall could not speak to him. She looked at him and waited for him to move a step closer. A

30

child who was standing in front of him said something, but the woman did not answer. When a policeman who had come up from behind got close enough to the fruit stall, she spoke to him immediately.

There was no phone box in the village. Bloch tried to call a friend from the post office. He waited on a bench near the switchboard, but the call did not go through. At that time of day the lines were busy, he was told. He swore at the post-mistress and walked out.

When, outside the village, he passed the swimming pool, he saw two policemen on bicycles coming towards him. "With capes," he thought. In fact, when the policemen stopped in front of him, they really were wearing capes; and when they got off their bicycles they did not even take the clips off their trousers. Again it seemed to Bloch as if he were watching a musical clock; as though he had seen all this before. He had not let go of the door in the fence that led to the pool even though it was closed. "The pool is closed," Bloch said.

The policemen, who made the usual remarks, nevertheless seemed to mean something entirely different by them; anyway they deliberately mispronounced phrases like "got to remember" and "go away" as "goats you remember" and "roadway" and saying "right is it" instead of "in the right" and "locked up" instead of "looked up". For what would be the point of telling him about the goats that, he should remember, had once, when the door had been left open, forced their way into the pool and had jumped right in it, which was why Bloch should leave the door locked up and stay in the roadway? As if to show their contempt for him, the policemen also failed to give their customary salutes when they rode away – or anyway, only hinted at them, as if they were hinting at something. They did not look back over their shoulders. To show that he had nothing to hide, Bloch stayed by the fence and went on looking in at the empty pool. "As if into an open wardrobe which I wanted to get something out of," Bloch thought. He could not remember now what he had

31

gone to the pool for. Besides, it was getting dark; the various illuminated signs on the outskirts of the village were already switched on. Bloch walked back into the village. When two girls ran past him toward the railway station, he called after them. Running, they turned round and shouted back. Bloch was hungry. He ate at the hotel; in the next room the television could already be heard. Later he took a glass in there and watched until the text card came on at the end of the programmes. He asked for his key and went upstairs. Half asleep, he thought he heard a car driving up outside with its headlights turned off. He asked himself why he had thought it had to be a car without lights; he must have fallen asleep in the middle of working it out.

Bloch was wakened by a banging and wheezing on the street, dustbins being tipped into the dust-cart; but when he looked out, he saw that the folding door of the bus that was just leaving had closed and, further away, that milk cans were being set on the loading ramp of the dairy. There weren't any dust-carts out here in the country; the confusion was starting all over again.

Bloch saw the girl in the doorway with a pile of towels on her arm and a torch on top of it; even before he could get her attention she was back out in the hall. Only after the door was closed did she excuse herself, but Bloch did not hear what she said because at the same time he was shouting something to her. He followed her out into the hall; she was already in another room. Back in his room, Bloch locked the door, giving the key two emphatic turns. Later he followed the girl, who by then had moved several rooms further on, and explained that it had been a misunderstanding. While putting a towel on the sink, the girl answered yes, it was a misunderstanding; before, from far away, she must have mistaken the bus driver on the stairs for him, so she had started into his room thinking that he had already gone downstairs. Bloch, who was standing in the open door, said that that was not what he had meant. But she had just turned

32

on the tap, so that she asked him to repeat what he had said. Then Bloch answered that there were far too many wardrobes and chests of drawers in the rooms. The girl answered yes, and as far as that went, there were far too few people working at the hotel, as the earlier mistake, which could be blamed on her exhaustion, just went to prove. That was not what he meant by his remark about wardrobes, answered Bloch, it was just that you couldn't move around easily in the rooms. The girl asked what he meant by that. Bloch did not answer. She replied to his silence by crumpling up the dirty towel – or, rather, Bloch assumed that her crumpling up of the towel was a response to his silence. She let the towel drop into the basket; again Bloch did not answer, which made her, so he believed, open the curtains, so that he quickly stepped back into the dim hallway. "That's not what I meant to say," the girl called. She came into the hall after him, but then Bloch followed her while she distributed towels in other rooms. At a bend in the hallway they came upon a pile of used bedsheets lying on the floor. When Bloch moved to avoid them, a soap packet fell from the top of the girl's pile of towels. Did she need a torch on the way home? asked Bloch. She had a boyfriend, answered the girl, who was straightening up with a flushed face. Did the hotel also have rooms with two sets of doors? asked Bloch. "My boyfriend is a carpenter, after all," answered the girl. He'd seen a film where a hotel thief got caught between such double doors, Bloch said. "Nothing's ever been taken from our rooms!" said the girl.

Downstairs in the dining room he read that a small American coin had been found beside the cashier, a nickel. The cashier's friends had never seen her with an American soldier, nor were there many American tourists in the country at this time. Furthermore, scribbles had been discovered in the margin of a newspaper, the kind of doodles someone might make while talking. The scribbling plainly was not the girl's; investigations were being made to determine whether it might reveal anything about her visitor.

33

The proprietor came to the table and put the registration form in front of him; he said that it had been lying in Bloch's room all the time. Bloch filled in the form. The proprietor stood at a slight distance and watched him. Just then the chain-saw in the sawmill outside bit into the timber. To Bloch the noise sounded like something forbidden.

Instead of just taking the form behind the bar, which would have been the natural thing to do, the proprietor took it into the next room and, as Bloch could see, spoke to his mother; then, instead of coming straight back again, as might be expected since the door had been left open, he went on talking and finally closed the door. Instead of the proprietor, the old woman came out. The proprietor did not come out after her but stayed in the room and pulled open the curtains, and then, instead of turning the television off, he turned on the extractor fan.

The girl now came into the dining room from the other side with a vacuum cleaner. Bloch fully expected to see her casually step out on to the street with the machine; instead, she plugged it into the socket and then pushed it back and forth under the tables and chairs. And when the proprietor closed the curtains in the next room, and, finally, the proprietor turned the fan off, it seemed to Bloch as if everything was falling back into place.

He asked the proprietor if the local people read many newspapers. "Only the weeklies and magazines," the innkeeper answered. Bloch, who was asking this while leaving, got his arm caught between the door handle and the door because he was pushing the handle down with his elbow. "That's what you get for that!" the girl shouted after him. Bloch could still hear the proprietor asking what she meant.

He wrote a few postcards but did not post them right away. Later, outside the village, when he wanted to stuff them into a postbox fastened to a fence, he noticed that the postbox would not be emptied again until tomorrow. Ever since his team, while touring South America, had had to send postcards to the newspapers with every member's signature on them, Bloch was in the habit, when he was on the road, of writing postcards.

A class of schoolchildren came by; the children were singing and Bloch pushed the cards in. The empty postbox resounded as they fell into it. But the box was so tiny that nothing could resound in it. Anyway, Bloch had walked away immediately.

He walked across country for a while. The feeling that a ball heavy with rain was dropping on his head gradually disappeared. Near the border the woods started. He turned back when he recognized the first watchtower on the other side of the no-man's-land clearing. At the edge of the woods he sat down on a tree trunk. He got up again immediately. Then he sat down again and counted his money. He looked up. The landscape, even though it was flat, curved toward him so firmly that it seemed to dislodge him. He was here at the edge of the woods, the electricity sub-station was over there, the milk stand was over there, a field was over there, a few people were over there, there he was at the edge of the woods. He sat as still as he could until he was not aware of himself any more. Later he realized that the people in the field were policemen with dogs.

Next to a blackberry bush, half hidden beneath the blackberries, Bloch found a child's bicycle. He stood it upright. The seat was screwed up quite high, as though for an adult. A few blackberry thorns were stuck in the tyres, though no air had escaped. The wheel was blocked by a fir branch that had been caught in the spokes. Bloch tugged at the branch. Then he dropped the bicycle, feeling that the policemen might, from far away, see the sun's reflections off the casing of the headlamp. But the policemen and their dogs had moved on.

Bloch looked after the figures running down an embankment; the dogs' name-tags and the walkie-talkies glinted. Did the glinting mean anything? Gradually it lost its significance: further away the headlight casings of cars flashed where the road turned a bend, a splinter from a pocket mirror sparkled

35

next to Bloch, and then the path glimmered with mica gravel. The gravel slid away under the tyres when Bloch got on the bicycle.

He rode a little way. Finally he leaned the bicycle against the sub-station and went on on foot.

He read the cinema poster that had been stuck on the milk stand with drawing-pins; the other posters under it had been torn away. Bloch walked on and saw a boy who had hiccups standing in a farmyard. He saw wasps flying around in an orchard. At a wayside crucifix there were rotting flowers in tin cans. In the grass at the side of the road lay empty cigarette boxes. Next to the closed windows he saw hooks hanging from the shutters. As he walked by an open window, he smelled something decayed. At the pub the landlady told him that somebody in the house opposite had died yesterday.

When Bloch went to join her in the kitchen, she met him at the door and walked ahead of him into the bar. Bloch passed her and walked towards a table in the corner, but she had already sat down at a table near the door. When Bloch was about to start talking, she beat him to it. He wanted to show her that the barmaid was wearing orthopaedic shoes, but the landlady was already pointing to the road outside, where a policeman was walking past, pushing a child's bicycle. "That bike belongs to the boy who can't talk," she said.

The barmaid had joined them, with a magazine in her hand; they all looked out of the window together. Bloch asked whether the well-digger had reported back. The landlady, who had understood only the words "reported back", started to talk about soldiers. Bloch said "come back" instead, and the landlady talked about the mute schoolboy. "He couldn't even call for help," the barmaid said, or rather read from a caption in the magazine. The landlady talked about a film where some nails had been mixed into cake dough. Bloch asked whether the guards on the watchtowers had field glasses; anyway, something was glinting up there. "You can't even see the watchtowers from here," answered one of the two women.

36

Bloch could see that they had flour on their faces from making cake, particularly on their eyebrows and at their hairlines.

He walked out into the yard, but when nobody came after him he went back inside. He stood by the juke box, leaving some room beside him. The barmaid, who was now sitting behind the bar, had broken a glass. The landlady had come out of the kitchen at the sound but, instead of looking at the barmaid, had looked at him. Bloch turned down the volume control on the back of the juke box. Then, while the landlady was still in the doorway, he turned the volume up again. The landlady walked in front of him through the bar as though she were pacing it off. Bloch asked her how much rent the estate owner charged for the pub. At this question Hertha stopped short. The barmaid swept the broken glass into a dustpan. Bloch walked towards Hertha, the landlady walked past him into the kitchen. Bloch went in after her.

Since the second chair was occupied by a cat, Bloch stood right next to her. She was talking about the estate owner's son, who was her boyfriend. Bloch stationed himself by the window and questioned her about him. She explained what the estate owner's son did. Without being asked, she went on talking. At the edge of the stove Bloch noticed a second preserving jar. Now and then he said, Yes? He noticed a second ruler in the overalls on the doorframe. He interrupted her to ask what number she started counting at. She hesitated, even stopped coring the apple. Bloch said that recently he had noticed that he himself was in the habit of starting to count only at the number two; this morning, for instance, he'd almost been run down by a car when he was crossing the street because he thought he had enough time until the second car; he'd simply not counted the first one. The landlady answered with a commonplace remark.

Bloch walked over to the chair and lifted it from behind so that the cat jumped down. He sat down but pushed the chair away from the table. In doing this, he bumped against a serving table, and a beer bottle fell down and rolled under the

37

kitchen sofa. Why was he always sitting down, getting up, going out, standing around, coming back in? asked the landlady. Was he doing it to tease her? Instead of answering, Bloch read her a joke from the newspaper under the apple parings. Since from where he sat the paper was upside down, he read so haltingly that the landlady, leaning forward, took over the job. Outside, the barmaid laughed. Inside, in the bedroom, something fell on the floor. No second sound followed. Bloch, who had not heard a sound the first time either, wanted to go and see; but the landlady explained that earlier she had heard the little girl waking up; she had just got out of bed and would probably come in any minute now and ask for a piece of cake. But Bloch then actually heard a sound likc whimpering. It turned out that the child had fallen out of bed in her sleep and couldn't work out where she was. In the kitchen the girl said there were some flies under her pillow. The landlady explained to Bloch that the neighbour's children, who, because of the death in their family, were sleeping over here for the duration of the wake, passed the time by shooting the rubber rings from preserving jars at flies on the wall; in the evening they put the flies that had fallen on the floor under the pillow.

After a few things had been pressed into the girl's hand – the first one or two she dropped again – she gradually calmed down. Bloch saw the barmaid come out of the bedroom with her hand cupped and toss the flies into the dustbin. It wasn't his fault, he said. He saw the baker's van stop in front of the neighbour's house and the driver put two loaves on the doorstep, the dark loaf on the bottom, the white one on top. The landlady sent the little girl to meet the driver at the door; Bloch heard the barmaid running water over her hand at the bar; lately he was always apologizing, the landlady said. Really? asked Bloch. Just then the little girl came into the kitchen with two loaves. He could also see the barmaid wiping her hands on her apron as she walked toward a customer. What did he want to drink? Who? Nothing right now, was the answer. The child had closed the door to the bar.

"Now we're alone," said Hertha. Bloch looked at the little girl standing by the window looking at the neighbour's house. "That doesn't count," she said. Bloch took this as a hint that she had something to tell him, but then he realized that what she had meant was that he should start talking. Bloch could not think of anything. He said something obscene. She immediately sent the child out of the room. He placed his hand beside hers. She told him off, softly. Roughly, he grabbed her arm but let go again immediately. Outside on the road he bumped into the child, who was poking a piece of straw into the plaster on the wall of the house.

He looked through the open window into the neighbour's house. On a trestle table he saw the corpse; next to it stood the coffin. A woman sat on a stool in the corner and dunked some bread into a cider jar; a young man lay asleep on his back on a bench behind the table; on his stomach lay a cat.

As Bloch came into the house, he almost fell over a log in the hallway. The woman came to the door; he stepped inside and talked with her. The young man had sat up but did not say anything; the cat had run out. "He had to keep watch all night," the woman said. In the morning she had found him quite drunk. She turned around to the dead man and said a prayer. Now and then she changed the water in the flowers. "It happened very quickly," she said. "We had to wake up our little boy so that he could run into the village." But then the child hadn't even been able to tell the priest what had happened, and so the bells hadn't been rung. Bloch realized that the room was being heated; after a while the wood in the stove had collapsed. "Go and get some more wood," said the woman. The young man came back with several logs, some under each arm, which he dropped down next to the stove so that the dust flew.

He sat down at the table, and the woman threw the logs into the stove. "We already lost one of our kids; he had pumpkins thrown at him," she said. Two old women went by outside the window and called in. On the windowsill Bloch noticed a black handbag. It had just been bought; the tissue paper stuffing had not even been taken out yet. "All of a sudden he gave a loud snore and died," the woman said.

Bloch could see into the bar opposite; the sun, which was quite low by now, shone so far into the room that the bottom part of it, especially the surfaces of the freshly waxed floorboards and the legs of the chairs, tables, and people, glowed as though of themselves. In the kitchen he could see the estate owner's son, who, leaning against the door with his arms across his chest, was talking to the landlady, who, presumably, was still sitting further away at the table. The deeper the sun sank, the deeper and more remote these images seemed to Bloch. He could not look away; only the children running back and forth on the road swept away the impression. A child came in with a bunch of flowers. The woman put the flowers in a tumbler and set the glass at the foot of the trestle. The child just stood there. After a while the woman handed her a coin and she went out.

Bloch heard a noise as if somebody had broken through the floorboards. But it was just the logs in the stove collapsing again. As soon as Bloch had stopped talking to the woman, the young man had stretched out on the bench and fallen back to sleep. Later several women came and told their beads. Somebody wiped the chalk marks off the blackboard outside the grocery shop and wrote instead: oranges, caramels, sardines. The conversation in the room was soft; the children outside were making a lot of noise. A bat had caught itself in the curtain; roused by the squeaking, the young man had leaped up and rushed toward it instantly, but the bat had already flown out.

It was the kind of dusk when no one felt like turning on the lights.

Only the bar across the street was faintly lit by the light from the juke box; but no records were playing. The kitchen was already dark. Bloch was invited to stay for supper and ate at the table with the others.

Although the window was now closed, gnats flew around the room. A child was sent to the pub to get some beermats; they were then put on top of the glasses so the gnats wouldn't get in. One woman noticed that she had lost the pendant from her necklace. Everybody started to look for it. Bloch stayed at the table. After a while he was seized by a need to be the one who found it, and he joined the others. When the pendant was not to be found in the room, they went on looking for it in the hall. A shovel fell over – or, rather, Bloch caught it just before it fell over completely. The young man was using a torch in the search, the woman came in with an oil lamp. Bloch asked for the torch and went out onto the road. Bent over, he walked about peering at the gravel, but nobody came out after him. He heard somebody in the hall call out that the pendant had been found. Bloch refused to believe it and went on looking. Then he heard them starting to pray again through the window. He put the torch on the outside of the windowsill and went away.

Back in the village, Bloch sat down in a cafe and started watching a card game. He began to argue with the player he was sitting behind. The other players told Bloch to get lost. Bloch went into the back room. A slide lecture was going on. Bloch watched for a while. It was a lecture on missionary hospitals in Southeast Asia. Bloch, who was making loud interruptions, started arguing with people again. He turned round and walked out.

He thought about going back inside, but he could not think of anything to say if he did. He went to the second cafe. There he asked to have the fan turned off. What's more, the lights were much too dim, he said. When the waitress sat down with him, after a time he made as if to put his arm around her; she realized that he was only kidding and leaned back even before he could make it clear to her that he had only been kidding. Bloch wanted to justify himself by really putting his arm around the waitress, but she had already stood up. When

Bloch wanted to get up, the waitress walked away. Now Bloch should have pretended that he wanted to follow her. But he had had enough, and he left the cafe.

In his room at the hotel he woke up just before dawn. All at once, everything around him was unbearable. He wondered whether he had woken just because at a certain moment, shortly before dawn, everything all at once became unbearable. The mattress he was lying on had caved in, the wardrobes and chests of drawers stood far away against the walls, the ceiling overhead was unbearably high. It was so quiet in the half-dark room, out in the hall, and especially out in the street, that Bloch could not stand it any longer. A fierce nausea gripped him. He vomited into the sink. He went on vomiting for a while, with no relief. He lay back down on the bed. He was not dizzy; on the contrary, he saw everything with excruiating stability. It did not help to lean out of the window and look along the road. A tarpaulin lay motionless over a parked car. Inside the room he noticed the two water pipes along the wall; they ran parallel to each other, cut off above by the ceiling and below by the floor. Everything he saw was cut off in the most unbearable way. The nausea did not so much elate him as depress him even more. It seemed as though a crowbar had pried him away from what he saw – or, rather, as though the things around him had all been pulled away from him. The wardrobe, the wash-basin, the suitcase, the door: only now did he realise that, as if in the grip of compulsion, he was thinking of the word for each thing. Each glimpse of a thing was immediately followed by its word. The chair, the clothes-hangers, the key. It had now become so quiet that no noises could distract him now; and because it had grown, on the one hand, so light that he could see the things all around him and, on the other hand, so quiet that no sound could distract him from them, he had seen the things as though they were, at the same time, advertisements for themselves. In fact, his nausea was the same kind of nausea that had sometimes been brought on by certain jingles, pop songs, or national anthems that he felt compelled to repeat word for word or hum to himself until he fell asleep. He held his breath as though he had hiccups. When he took another breath, it came back. He held his breath again. After a while this began to help, and he fell asleep.

The next morning he could not imagine any of that any more. The dining room had already been done out, and a tax inspector was walking round while the proprietor told him the prices of everything. The proprietor told him the prices of everything. The proprietor showed the inspector the receipts for the coffee-machine and a freezer; the fact that the two men were discussing prices made his state during the night seem all the more ridiculous to Bloch. He had put the newspapers aside after quickly leafing through them and was now listening only to the tax inspector, who was arguing with the proprietor about the price of an ice-cream freezer. The proprietor's mother and the girl joined them; all of them talked at once. Bloch broke in to ask what the furnishings for one room in the hotel might cost. The proprietor answered that he had bought the furniture quite cheap from nearby farmers who had either moved away or left the country altogether. He told Bloch a price. Bloch wanted that price broken down item by item. The proprietor asked the girl for the inventory list for a room and gave the price he had paid for each item as well as the price he thought he could get for a chest or a wardrobe. The tax inspector, who had been taking notes up to that point, stopped writing and asked the girl for a glass of wine. Bloch, satisfied, was ready to leave. The tax inspector explained that whenever he saw an item, say a washing-machine, he always asked the price immediately, and then when he saw the item again, say a washing-machine of the same make, he would recognize it not by its external features, that is, a washing-machine by the knobs which regulated the washing programme, but by what the item, say a washing-machine, had cost when he first saw it, that is, by its price. The price, of course, he remembered precisely, and that way he could recognize almost any item. And

43

what if the item was worthless, asked Bloch. He had nothing to do with items that had no market value, the inspector replied, at least not in his work.

The mute schoolboy still had not been found. Though the bicycle had been impounded and the surrounding area was being searched, the shot that might have been the signal that one of the policemen had come across something had not been fired. Anyway, in the barber's where Bloch had gone, the noise of the hair-dryer behind the screen was so loud that he could not hear anything from outside. He asked to have the hair at the back of his neck clipped. While the barber was washing his hands, the girl brushed off Bloch's collar. Now the hair-dryer was turned off and he heard paper rustling behind the screen. There was a bang. But it was only a curler that had fallen into a metal pan behind the screen.

Bloch asked the girl if she went home for lunch. The girl answered that she didn't live in the village, she came every morning by train; for lunch she went to a cafe or stayed with the other girl here in the shop. Bloch asked whether she bought a return ticket every day. The girl told him that she commuted on a weekly ticket. "How much is a weekly ticket?" Bloch asked immediately. But before the girl could answer, he said that it was none of his business. Nevertheless, the girl told him the price. From behind the screen the other girl said, "Why are you asking if it's none of your business?" Bloch, who was already standing up waiting for his change, read the price list next to the mirror, and went out.

He noticed that he had an odd compulsion to find out the price of everything. He was actually relieved to see the prices of newly arrived goods marked on the window of a grocery shop. On a fruit display in front of the shop a price tag had fallen over. He set it right. The movement was enough to bring somebody out to ask if he wanted to buy something. At another shop a rocking chair had been covered by a long dress. A tag with a pin stuck through it lay on the chair next to the dress. Bloch was long undecided whether the price was for the

44

chair or for the dress; one or the other must not be for sale. He stood so long in front of them that, again, somebody came out and questioned him. He questioned back. He was told that the price tag with the pin must have fallen off the dress; it was clear, wasn't it, that the tag couldn't have anything to do with the chair; naturally, that was private property. He had just wanted to ask, said Bloch, moving on. The other person called after him to tell him where he could buy that kind of rocking chair. In the cafe Bloch asked the price of the juke box. It didn't belong to him, said the owner, he just leased it. That's not what he meant, Bloch answered, he just wanted to know the price. Not until the owner had told him the price was Bloch satisfied. But he wasn't sure, the owner said. Bloch now began to ask about other things in the cafe that the owner had to know the prices of because they were his. The owner then talked about the public swimming pool, which had cost much more than the original estimate. "How much more?" Bloch asked. The owner didn't know. Bloch became impatient. "And what was the estimate?" asked Bloch. Again the owner didn't have the answer. Anyway, last spring a corpse had been found in one of the cubicles; it must have been lying there all winter. The head was stuck in a plastic shopping bag. The dead man had been a gypsy. Some gypsies had settled in this region; with the reparation money they'd received for being confined in the concentration camps, they'd built themselves little houses at the edge of the woods. "They're supposed to be very clean inside," the owner said. The policemen who had questioned the inhabitants during their search for the missing boy had been surprised by the freshly scrubbed floors and the general neatness of the rooms everywhere. But it was just that neatness, the owner went on, that actually fed their suspicions, for the gypsies certainly wouldn't have scrubbed the floors without good reason. Bloch carried on and asked whether the reparations had been enough to cover the cost of building the houses. The owner couldn't say what the reparations had amounted to. "Building materials and labour were still cheap in those days," the owner said. Out of curiosity Bloch turned over the sales slip that was stuck to the bottom of the beer glass. "Is this worth anything?" he asked, reaching into his pocket and putting a stone on the table. Without picking up the stone the owner answered that you could find stones like that at every step around there. Bloch said nothing. Then the owner picked up the stone, let it roll around the hollow of his hand, and set it back on the table. Finished! Bloch promptly put the stone away.

In the doorway he met the two girls from the barber's. He invited them to go with him to the other cafe. The second girl said that the juke box there didn't have any records. Bloch asked what she meant. She told him that the records in the juke box were no good. Bloch went ahead and they followed after him. They ordered something to drink and unwrapped their sandwiches. Bloch leaned forward and chatted with them. They showed him their identity cards. When he touched the plastic covers, his hands immediately began to sweat. They asked him if he was a soldier. The second one had a date that night with a travelling salesman; but they'd make it a foursome because there was nothing to talk about when there were only two of you. "When there are four of you, somebody will say something, then somebody else. You can tell each other jokes." Bloch did not know what to answer. In the next room a baby was crawling about on the floor. A dog was bounding around the child and licking its face. The telephone on the counter rang; as long as it was ringing, Bloch stopped listening to the conversation. Soldiers mostly didn't have any money, one of the girls said. Bloch did not answer. When he looked at their hands, they explained that their fingernails were so black because of the hairsetting lotion. "It doesn't help to polish them, the tips always stay black." Bloch looked up. "We buy all our dresses ready-made." "We do each other's hair." "In the summer it's usually getting light by the time we finally get home." "I prefer the slow dances." "On the trip home we don't joke around as much any more, then we forget about

46

talking." She took everything too seriously, the first girl said. Yesterday on the way to the station she had even looked in the orchard for the missing schoolboy. Instead of handing back their identity cards, Bloch just put them down on the table, as if it hadn't been right for him to look at them. He watched the dampness of his fingerprints evaporate from the plastic. When they asked him what he did, he told them that he had been a goalkeeper. He explained that goalkeepers could go on playing longer than other players. "Zamora was already quite old," said Bloch. In an answer, they talked about the football players they had known personally. When there was a game in their town, they stood behind the visiting team's goal and heckled the goalie to make him nervous. Most goalies were bow-legged.

Bloch noticed that each time he mentioned something and talked about it, the two of them countered with a story about their own experiences with the same or a similar thing or with a story they had heard about it. For instance, if Bloch talked about the ribs he had broken while playing, they told him that a few days ago one of the workers at the sawmill had fallen off a timber stack and broken his ribs; and if Bloch then mentioned that his lips had had to be stitched more than once, they answered by talking about a fight on television in which a boxer's eyebrow had been split open; and when Bloch told how once he had slammed into a goalpost during a lunge and split his tongue, they immediately replied that the missing schoolboy also had a cleft tongue.

Besides, they talked about things and especially about people he couldn't possibly know as though he did know them, was one of their group. Maria had hit Otto over the head with her crocodile-skin handbag. Uncle had come down into the cellar, chased Alfred into the yard, grabbed the Italian cook and beaten her with a birch rod. Eduard had dropped her where the road forked, so that she had to walk the rest of the way in the middle of the night; she had to go through Hangman's Wood, so that Walter and Karl wouldn't see her on

Lovers' Lane, and she'd finally taken off the dancing shoes Herr Friedrich had given her. Bloch, on the other hand, explained, whenever he mentioned a name, whom he was talking about. Even when he mentioned an object, he described it so as to make it clear.

When the name Viktor came up, Bloch added, "a friend of mine", and when he talked about an indirect free kick, he not only described what an indirect free kick was but explained, while the girls waited for the story to go on, the general rules about free kicks. When he mentioned a corner kick that had been awarded by a referee, he even felt he owed them the explanation that he was not talking about the corner of a room. The longer he talked, the less natural what he said seemed to Bloch. Gradually it began to seem that every word needed an explanation. He had to watch himself so that he didn't get stuck in the middle of a sentence. A couple of times when he thought out a sentence even while he said it, he made a slip of the tongue; when what the girls were saying ended exactly as he thought it would, he couldn't answer at first. As long as they had gone on with this familiar talk, he had also forgotten the surroundings more and more; he had even stopped noticing the child and the dog in the next room; but when he began to hesitate and did not know how to go on and finally searched for sentences he might still say, the surroundings became conspicuous again, and he noticed details everywhere. Finally he asked whether Alfred was her boyfriend; whether the birch rod was always kept on top of the wardrobe; whether Herr Friedrich was a travelling salesman; and whether perhaps Hangman's Wood was called that because there really had been a gallows there once. They answered readily; and gradually, instead of bleached hair with dark roots, instead of the single brooch at the neck, instead of a black-rimmed fingernail, instead of the single pimple on the shaved eyebrow, instead of the split lining of the empty cafe chair, Bloch once again became aware of contours, movements, voices, exclamations, and figures all together.

And with a single sure rapid movement he also caught the handbag that had suddenly slipped off the table. The first girl offered him a bite of her sandwich, and when she held it toward him he bit into it as though this was the most natural thing in the world.

Outside, he heard that the schoolchildren had been given the day off so that they could all look for the boy. But all they found were a couple of things that, except for a broken mirror, had nothing to do with the missing child. The plastic cover of the mirror had identified it as the boy's property. Even though the area where the mirror was discovered had been carefully searched, no other clues were found. The policeman who was telling Bloch all this added that the whereabouts of one of the gypsies had remained unknown since the day of the disappearance. Bloch was surprised that the policeman, who was still on the other side of the road, bothered to stop and shout all this information over to him. He called back to ask if the swimming pool had been searched yet. The policeman answered that the pool was locked; nobody could get in there not even a gypsy.

Outside the village, Bloch noticed that the fields of maize had been almost completely trampled down, so that yellow pumpkin blossoms were visible between the bent stalks; in the middle of the field, always in the shade, the pumpkins had only now begun to blossom. Broken corncobs, partially peeled and gnawed by the schoolchildren, were scattered all over the road; the black silk that had been torn off the cobs lay next to them. Even in the village Bloch had watched the children throwing balls of the black fibres at each other while they waited for the bus. The cornsilk was so wet that every time Bloch stepped on it, it squashed as though he were walking across marshy ground. He almost tripped over a weasel that had been run over; its tongue had been squeezed some way out of its mouth. Bloch stopped and, with the tip of his shoe, touched the long slim tongue, black with blood; it was hard and rigid. He kicked the weasel to the side of the road

49

and walked on.

At the bridge he left the road and walked along the brook towards the border. Gradually, the brook seemed to become deeper; anyway, the water flowed more and more slowly. The hazelnut bushes on both sides hung so far over the brook that the surface was barely visible. Some distance away, a scythe was swishing as it moved. The slower the water flowed, the muddier it seemed to become. Approaching a bend, the brook stopped flowing altogether, and the water became completely opaque. From far away there was the sound of a tractor clattering as though it had nothing to do with any of this. Black bunches of overripe blackberries hung in the thicket. Tiny oil flecks floated on the still surface of the water.

Bubbles could be seen rising from the bottom of the water every so often. The tips of the hazelnut bushes hung into the brook. Now there was no outside sound to distract attention. The bubbles had scarcely reached the surface when they disappeared again. Something leaped out so quickly that you couldn't tell if it had been a fish.

When after a while Bloch moved suddenly, a gurgling sound ran through the water. He stepped onto a footbridge that led across the brook and, motionless, looked down at the water. The water was so still that the tops of the leaves floating on it stayed completely dry.

Water bugs were dashing back and forth, and above them you could see, without lifting your head, a swarm of gnats. At one spot the water rippled ever so slightly. There was another splash as a fish leaped out of the water. At the edge, you could see one toad sitting on top of another. A clump of earth came loose from the shore, and there was another bubbling under the water. The minute events on the water's surface seemed so important that when they recurred you simultaneously observed them and committed them to memory. And the leaves moved so slowly on the water that you felt like watching them without blinking, until your eyes hurt, for fear that you might mistake the movement of your eyelids for the movement of the leaves. Not even the branches almost dipping into the muddy water were reflected in it.

Outside his field of vision something began to bother Bloch, who was staring fixedly at the water. He blinked as if it was his eyes' fault but did not look around. Gradually it came into his field of vision. For a while he saw it without really taking it in; his whole consciousness seemed to be a blind spot. Then, as when in a comedy film somebody casually opens a box and goes on talking, and then does a double-take and rushes back to the box, he saw below him in the water the corpse of a child.

He had then gone back to the road. On the bend where the last houses before the border stood, a policeman on a motor-bike was coming towards him. Bloch had already seen him in the roadside mirror that stood on the bend. Then he really appeared, sitting up straight on his bike, wearing white gloves, one hand on the handlebars, the other on his stomach; the tyres were spattered with mud. The policeman's face revealed nothing. The longer Bloch gazed after the figure of the police-man on the bike, the more it seemed to him that he was slowly looking up from a newspaper and through a window out into the open: the policeman moved further and further away and mattered less and less to him. At the same time, it struck Bloch that what he saw while gazing after the policeman looked for a moment like a simile for something else. The policeman disappeared out of the picture, and Bloch's atten-tion grew completely superficial. In the pub by the border, where he went next, he found no one at first, though the door to the bar was open.

He stood there for a while, then opened the door again and closed it carefully from the inside. He sat down at a table in the corner and passed the time by playing about with the little counters used for keeping score in card games. Finally he shuffled the pack of cards that had been stuck between the rows of counters and played a game by himself. He became totally immersed in the game; a card fell under the table. He bent down and saw the landlady's little girl squatting under

51

another table, between the chairs that had been set all round it. Bloch straightened up and went on playing; the pack was so worn that each individual card seemed swollen. He could see into the room of the neighbour's house, where the trestle table was not empty; the casement windows stood wide open. Children were shouting on the road outside, and the girl under the table hastily pushed away the chairs and ran out.

The barmaid came in from the yard. As if she were answering his sitting there, she said the landlady had gone to the castle to have the lease renewed. The barmaid had been followed by a young man dragging two crates of beer bottles, one in each hand; even so, his mouth was not closed. Bloch spoke to him, but the barmaid said he shouldn't, because he couldn't talk when he was pulling such heavy loads. The young man, who, it seemed, was slightly feeble-minded, had stacked the crates behind the bar. The barmaid said to him: 'Is he pouring the ashes on the bed again instead of into the brook? Has he stopped jumping at the goats? He has started cutting open pumpkins again and smearing the stuff all over his face?" She stood next to the door, holding a beer bottle, but he did not answer. When she showed him the bottle, he came toward her. She gave him the bottle and let him out. A cat dashed in, leaped at a fly in the air, and gulped down the fly at once. The barmaid had closed the door. While the door had been open, Bloch had heard the phone ringing in the customs shed next door.

Following close behind the young man, Bloch then went up to the castle. He walked slowly because he did not want to catch up with him; he watched him as he pointed excitedly up into a pear tree and heard him say, "Swarm of bees," and at first believed that he saw a swarm of bees hanging there until he realized, after looking at the other trees, that it was just that the trunks had thickened at some points. He saw the young man hurl the beer bottle up into the tree, as if to prove that it was bees that he saw. The dregs of the beer sprayed against the trunk, the bottle fell onto a heap of rotting pears in

52

the grass; flies and wasps immediately swarmed up out of the pears. As Bloch came alongside the young man, he heard him talking about the "bathing nutcase" he'd seen swimming in the brook yesterday; his fingers had been all shrivelled up, and there was a big bubble of foam in front of his mouth. Bloch asked him if he himself knew how to swim. He saw the young man force his mouth open wide and nod emphatically, but then he heard him say, "No." Bloch walked on ahead and could hear him still talking but did not look back again.

Outside the castle, he knocked on the window of the gatekeeper's cottage. He went up so close to the pane that he could see inside. There was a basin full of plums on the table. The gatekeeper, who was lying on the sofa, had just wakened; he made signs that Bloch did not know how to answer. He nodded. The gatekeeper came out with a key and opened the gate but immediately turned round again and walked ahead. "A gatekeeper with a key!" thought Bloch; again it seemed as if he should be seeing all this only in a figurative sense. He realized that the gatekeeper planned to show him round the building. He decided to clear up the confusion but, even though the gatekeeper did not say much, he never had the chance. The entrance door, through which they went, had fish-heads nailed all over it. Bloch had started on his explanation, but he must have missed the right moment again. They were inside already.

In the library the gatekeeper read to him from the estate books how many shares of the harvest the peasants used to have to turn over to the lord of the manor as rent. Bloch had no chance to interrupt him then, because the gatekeeper was just translating a Latin entry dealing with an insubordinate peasant. " 'He had to depart from the estate,' " the gate-keeper read, " 'and some time later he was discovered in the forest, hanging by his feet from a branch, his head in an ant-hill.' " The estate book was so thick that the gatekeeper had to use both hands to shut it. Bloch asked if the house was in-habited. The gatekeeper answered that visitors were not

53

allowed into the private quarters. Bloch heard a clicking sound, but it was just the gatekeeper locked the estate book back up. " 'The darkness in the fir forests,' " the gatekeeper recited from memory " 'had caused him to take leave of his senses.' " Outside the window there was a sound like a heavy apple coming loose from a branch. But nothing hit the ground. Bloch looked out of the window and saw the estate owner's son in the garden carrying a long pole; at the tip of the pole hung a sack with metal prongs that he used to pull apples off the tree and into the sack, while the landlady stood on the grass below with her apron spread out.

On the walls of the next room were hanging cases of butterflies. The gatekeeper showed him how stained his hands had become from preparing them. Even so, many of the butterflies had fallen off the pins that had held them in place; underneath the cases Bloch saw the dust on the floor. He stepped closer and inspected those butterflies that were still held in place by pins. When the gatekeeper closed the door behind him, something fell to the floor outside his field of vision and dissolved into dust even as it fell. Bloch saw an Emperor moth that seemed almost completely overgrown with a woolly green film. He did not ben forward or step back. He read the labels under the empty pins. Some of the butterflies had changed so much that they could be identified only by the descriptions. " 'A corpse in the living room,' "recited the gatekeeper, standing in the doorway to the next room. Outside, someone screamed, and an apple hit the ground. Bloch, looking out of the window, saw that an empty branch had snapped back. The landlady put the apple that had fallen to the ground onto the pile of other damaged apples.

Later on, a school class from outside the village joined them, and the gatekeeper interrupted his tour to begin it all over again. Bloch took this chance to leave.

Out on the road, he sat on a bench at the bus-stop that, as a brass plate on it attested, had been donated by the local savings bank. The houses were so far away that they could hardly be distinguished from each other; when bells began to toll, they could not be seen in the belfry. A plane flew overhead, so high that he could not see it; only once did it glint. Next to him on the bench there was a dried-up snail spoor. The grass under the bench was wet with last night's dew; the cellophane wrapper of a cigarette packet was fogged with mist. To his left he saw . . . To his right there was . . . Behind him he saw . . . He got hungry and walked on.

Back at the pub, Bloch ordered a cold snack. The barmaid, using an automatic bread-slicer, cut the bread and the sausage and brought him the sausage slices on a plate; she had squeezed some mustard on top. Bloch ate; it was getting dark already. Outside, one of the children playing hide-and-seek had hidden himself so well that no one had found him. Only after the game was over did Bloch see him walk along the deserted road. He pushed the plate aside, pushed the beermat aside as well, pushed the saltcellar away from himself.

The barmaid put the little girl to bed. Later the child came back into the bar in her nightgown and ran around among the customers. Every so often, moths fluttered up from the floor. After she came back, the landlady carried the child back into the bedroom.

The curtains were closed and the bar was full. Several young men were standing at the bar; every time they laughed, they took one step backward. Next to them stood girls in shot-silk coats, looking as if they wanted to leave again immediately. When one of the young men told a story, the others could be seen to stiffen up just before they all screamed with laughter. The people sitting down preferred to sit against the wall. The mechanical hand in the juke box could be seen grabbing a record and the playing arm coming down on it, and some people could be heard to quieten down as they waited for their records; it was no use, it didn't change anything. And it didn't change anything that when the barmaid let her arm drop you could see her wristwatch slip out from under her sleeve and down to her wrist, that the lever on the coffee machine rose

55

slowly, and that you could hear somebody hold a match-box to his ear and shake it before opening it. You saw how glasses empty long ago were repeatedly brought to the lips, how the barmaid lifted a glass to check whether she could take it away, how the young men pummelled each other's faces in fun. Nothing helped. Only when somebody shouted for his bill did things become real again.

Bloch was quite drunk. Everything seemed to be out of his reach. He was so far away from what was happening around him that he himself no longer appeared in what he saw and heard. "Like aerial photographs," he thought while looking at the antlers and horns on the wall. The noises seemed to him like static, like the coughing and clearing of throats during radio broadcasts of church services.

Later the estate owner's son came in. He was wearing knickerbockers; he hung his coat so close to Bloch that Bloch had to lean to one side.

The landlady sat down with the estate owner's son, and you could hear her asking him as she sat down what he wanted to drink and then shouting the order to the barmaid. For a while Bloch saw them both drinking from the same glass; whenever the young man said something, the landlady nudged him in the ribs; and when she swiped the flat of her hand across his face, he could be seen snapping at it and licking it. Then the landlady had sat down at another table, where she went on with her business-like routine by fingering another young man's hair. The estate owner's son had stood up again and reached for his cigarettes in the coat behind Bloch. When Bloch shook his head in answer to a question about whether the coat bothered him, he realized that he had not lifted his eyes from one and the same spot for quite a while. Bloch shouted, "Bill, please!" and everybody seemed to become serious again for a moment. The landlady, whose head was bent backward because she was just opening a bottle of wine, made a sign to the barmaid, who was standing behind the bar washing glasses, which she put on the foam-rubber mat that soaked up the water, and the barmaid walked towards him, between the young men standing at the bar, and gave him his change, with fingers that were cold, and as he stood up, he put the wet coins in his pocket immediately; a joke, thought Bloch; perhaps the sequence of events seemed so laborious to him because he was drunk.

He stood up and walked to the door; he opened the door and went outside – everything was all right.

Just to make sure, he stood there for a while. Every once in a while somebody came out to relieve himself. Others, who were just arriving, started to sing along as soon as they heard the juke box, even when they were still outside. Bloch moved off.

Back in the village; back at the hotel; back in his room. "Twelve words altogether," thought Bloch with relief. He heard bath water draining out overhead; anyway, he heard a gurgling, then a sucking, and finally the sound of a smacking kiss.

He must have just dropped off when he woke up again. For a moment it seemed as if he had fallen out of himself. He realized he was lying in a bed. "Not fit to be moved," thought Bloch. A cancer. He became aware of himself as if he had suddenly degenerated. He did not matter any more. No matter how still he lay, he was one big wriggling and retching; his lying there was so sharply distinct and glaring that he could not escape into even one image that he might have compared himself with. The way he lay there, he was something lewd, obscene, inappropriate, thoroughly obnoxious. "Bury it!" thought Bloch. "Prohibit it, remove it!" He thought he was touching himself unpleasantly but realized that his awareness of himself was so intense that he felt it like a sense of touch all over his body; as though his consciousness, as though his thoughts, had become palpable, aggressive, abusive toward himself. Defenceless, incapable of defending himself, he lay there. Nauseatingly his insides turned out; not alien, only repulsively different. It had been a jolt, and with one jolt he

57

had become unnatural, had been torn out of context. He lay there, as impossible as he was real; no comparisons now. His awareness of himself was so strong that he was scared to death. He was sweating. A coin fell on the floor and rolled under the bed: a comparison? Then he had fallen asleep.

Waking up again. "Two, three, four," Bloch started to count. His situation had not changed, but he must have grown used to it in his sleep. He pocketed the coin that had fallen under the bed and went downstairs. When he concentrated and took control of himself, one word still nicely yielded the next. A rainy October day; early morning; a dusty window-pane; it worked. He greeted the proprietor; the proprietor was just putting the newspapers into their racks; the girl was pushing a tray through the service hatch between the kitchen and dining room: it was still working. If he kept up his guard, it could go on like this, one thing after another; he sat at the table he always sat at; he opened the newspaper he opened every day; he read the paragraph in the paper that said an important lead in the Gerda T. case was being followed into the southern half of the country; the doodles in the margin of the newspaper that had been found in the dead girl's apart-ment had furthered the investigation. One sentence yielded the next sentence. And then, and then, and then . . . For a little while it was possible to look ahead without worrying.

After a time, although he was still sitting in the dining room listing the things that went on out on the road, Bloch caught himself becoming aware of a sentence, "For he had been idle too long." Since that sentence looked like a final sentence to Bloch, he thought back to how he had come to it. What had come before it? Oh, yes, earlier he had thought, "Surprised by the shot, he'd let the ball roll right through his legs." And before this sentence he had thought about the photographers who annoyed him behind the goal. And before that: "Some-body had stopped behind him but had only whistled for his dog." And before that sentence? Before that sentence he had thought about a woman who had stopped in a park, had

58

turned round, and had looked at something behind him the way one looks at an unruly child. And before that? Before that, the proprietor had talked about the mute schoolboy, who'd been found dead by a customs man just before the border. And before the schoolboy he had thought of the ball that had bounced up just in front of the goal line. And before the schoolboy he had thought of the ball that had bounced up just in front of the goal line. And before the thought of the ball, he had seen the market woman jump up from her stool on the street and run after a schoolboy. And the market woman had been preceded by a sentence in the paper: "The carpenter was hindered in his pursuit of the thief by the fact that he was still wearing his apron." But he had read the sentence in the paper just when he thought of how his jacket had been pulled down over his arms during a mugging. And he had thought of the mugging when he had hurt his shin against the table. And before that? He could not remember any more what had made him bump his shin against the table. He searched the sequence for a clue about what might have come before: did it have to do with the movement? or with the pain? or with the sound of table and shin? But it did not go any further back. Then he noticed, in the paper in front of him, a picture of a front door that, because there was a corpse behind it, had had to be broken open. So, he thought, it all started with this front door, until he had brought himself back to the sentence, "He had been idle too long."

Everything had gone well for a while after that: the lip movements of the people he talked to coincided with what he heard them say; the houses were not just facades; heavy sacks of flour were being dragged from the loading ramp of the dairy into the storage room; when somebody shouted something down below in the road, it actually sounded as though it came from down there. The people walking past on the opposite pavement did not appear to have been paid to walk past in the background; the man with the sticking plaster under his eye had a genuine scab; and the rain seemed to fall not just in the

59

foreground of the picture but everywhere. Bloch then found himself under the overhanging roof of a church. He must have got there through a side alley and stopped under the roof when it started to rain.

Inside the church he noticed that it was brighter than he had expected. So he was able, sitting straight down on a bench, to look up at the painted ceiling. After a while he recognized it: it was reproduced in the brochure that was placed in every room at the hotel. Bloch, who had brought a copy because it also contained a sketch-map of the village and its vicinity with all its roads and footpaths, pulled out the brochure and read that different painters had worked on the background and foreground of the picture; the figures in the foreground had been finished long before the other painter had finished filling in the background. Bloch looked from the page up into the vaulted roof; because he did not know them, the figures – they probably represented people from the Bible – bored him; still it was pleasant to look up at the roof while it rained harder and harder outside. The painting stretched all the way across the ceiling of the church. The background represented the sky, almost cloudless and an almost even blue; here and there a few fluffy clouds could be seen; at one spot, quite far above the figures, a bird had been painted. Bloch estimated the exact area the painter had had to fill with paint. Would it have been hard to paint such an even blue? It was a blue that was so light that white had probably been mixed into the colour. And in mixing it didn't you have to be careful that the shade of blue didn't change from day to day? On the other hand, the blue was not absolutely even but changed within each brush stroke. So you couldn't just paint the ceiling an even blue but actually had to paint a picture. The background did not become sky simply by slapping paint blindly on the plaster base – which, moreover, had to be wet – with as a big a brush as possible, maybe even with a broom; on the contrary, Bloch reflected, the painter had to paint an actual sky with small variations in the blue which, nevertheless, had to be so indistinct that nobody would think they were a mistake in the mixing. In fact, the background looked like a sky not because you were used to imagining a sky in the background, but because the sky had been painted there, stroke by stroke. It had been painted with such precision, thought Bloch, that it almost looked drawn; it was much more precise, anyway, than the figures in the foreground. Had he added the bird out of sheer rage? And had he painted the bird right at the start or had he only added it when he was quite finished? Might the background painter have been in some kind of despair? Nothing indicated this, and such an interpretation immediately seemed ridiculous to Bloch. Altogether it seemed to him as if his preoccupation with the painting, as if his walking back and forth, his sitting here and there, his going out, his coming in, were nothing but excuses. He stood up, "No distractions," he muttered to himself. As if to contradict himself, he went outside, walked straight across the road into an entrance way, and stood there defiantly among the empty milk bottles – not that anyone came to ask him to account for his presence there – until it stopped raining. Then he went to a cafe and sat there for a while with his legs stretched out – not that anyone did him the favour of stumbling over them and starting a fight.

When he looked out, he saw a segment of the marketplace with the school bus; in the cafe he saw, to the left and to the right, segments of the walls, one with an unlit stove with a bunch of flowers on it, the one on the other side with a coat rack and an umbrella hanging from it. He noticed another segment with the juke box with a point of light walking slowly across it before it stopped at the selected number, and next to it a cigarette machine with another bunch of flowers on top; then still another segment with the cafe owner behind the bar and next to him the waitress for whom he was opening a bottle, which the waitress put on the tray; and, finally, a segment of himself with his legs stretched out, the dirty toes of his wet shoes, and also the huge ashtray on the table and next to it

61

a vase, which was smaller, and the filled wine glass on the next table, where at that moment nobody was sitting. His angle of vision onto the square corresponded, as he realized now that the school bus had left, almost exactly with the angle on the picture postcards; here a segment of the memorial column by the fountain; there, at the edge of the picture, a segment of the bicycle stand.

Bloch was irritated. Within the segments themselves he saw details with grating distinctness: as if the parts he saw stood for the whole. Again the details seemed to him like nameplates. "Neon signs," he thought. So he saw the waitress's ear with one earring as a sign of the entire person; and a handbag on a nearby table, slightly open so that he could distinguish a polka-dot scarf in it, stood for the woman holding the coffee cup who was sitting behind it and, with her other hand, pausing only now and then at a picture, rapidly leafing through a magazine. A tower of ice-cream dishes dovetailed into each other on the bar seemed a simile for the cafe owner, and the puddle on the floor by the coat rack represented the umbrella hanging above it. Instead of the heads of the customers, Bloch saw the dirty spots on the wall at the level of their heads. He was so irritated that he looked at the grimy cord that the waitress was just pulling to turn off the wall lights – it had grown brighter outside again – as if the entire lighting arrangement was designed especially to challenge him. Also, his head hurt because he had been caught in the rain.

The grating details seemed to besmirch and completely distort the figures and the surroundings they fitted into. The only defence was to name the things one by one and use those names as insults against the people themselves. The owner behind the bar might be called an ice-cream dish, and you could tell the waitress that she was a pierced ear lobe. And you also felt like saying to the woman with the magazine, "You Handbag, you," and to the man at the next table, who had finally come out of the back room and, standing up, finished his wine while he paid, "You Stain on Your Trousers," or to shout

62

after him as he set the empty glass on the table and walked out that he was a fingerprint, a doorknob, the slit in the back of his coat, a rain puddle, a bicycle clip, a mudguard, and so on, until the figure outside had disappeared on his bicycle . . . Even the conversation and especially the exclamations – "What?" and "I see" – seemed so grating that you wanted to repeat the words out loud, scornfully.

Bloch went into a butcher's shop and bought two salami bread rolls. He did not want to eat at the pub because his money was running low. He looked over the sausages dangling together from a pole and pointed at the one he wanted the girl to slice. A boy came in with a note in his hand. At first the customs man thought the schoolboy's corpse was a mattress that had been washed up, the girl had just said. She took two rolls out of a carton and split them in half without separating them completely. The bread was so stale that Bloch heard them crunch as the knife cut into them. The girl pulled the rolls apart and put the sliced meat inside. Bloch said that he had time and she should serve the child first. He saw the boy silently holding the note out. The girl leaned forward and read it. Then when she was chopping off a piece of meat, it slipped off the board and fell onto the stone floor. "Plop," said the child. The meat had stayed where it had fallen. The girl picked it up, scraped it off with the edge of her knife, and wrapped it up. Outside, Bloch saw the schoolchildren walking by with their umbrellas open, even though it had stopped raining. He opened the door for the boy and watched the girl tear the skin off the sausage end and put the slices inside the second roll.

Business was bad, the girl said. "There aren't any houses except on this side of the road where the shop is, so that, first of all, nobody lives opposite who could see from there that there is a shop here and, second, the people going by never walk on the other side of the road, so they pass by so close that they don't see that there is a shop here either, especially since the shop window isn't much bigger than the livng-room windows of the houses next door."

Bloch wondered why the people didn't walk on the other side of the road as well, where there was more room and where it was sunnier. Probably everybody feels some need to walk right next to the houses, he said. The girl, who had not understood him because he had become disgusted with talking in the middle of the sentence and had only mumbled the rest, laughed as though all she had expected for an answer was a joke. In fact, when a few people passed by the shop window, it got so dark in the shop that it did seem like a joke.

"First of all . . . second . . ." Bloch repeated to himself what the girl had said; it seemed uncanny to him how someone could begin to speak and at the same time know how the sentence would end. Outside, he ate the rolls while he walked along. He screwed up the waxed paper they were wrapped in and was ready to throw it away. There was no litter bin nearby. For a while he walked along with the screwed up paper, first in one direction and then in another. He put the paper in his coat pocket, took it out again, and finally threw it through a fence into an orchard. Chickens came running from all directions at once but turned back before they had pecked the paper ball open.

In front of him Bloch saw three men walking diagonally across the street, two in uniform and the one in the middle in a black Sunday suit with a tie hanging over his shoulder, where it had been blown either by the wind or by fast running. He watched as the policeman led the gypsy into the police station. They walked next to each other as far as the door, and the gypsy, it seemed, moved easily and willingly between the two policemen and talked with them; when one of the policemen pushed open the door, the other did not grab the gypsy but just touched his elbow lightly from behind. The gypsy looked back over his shoulder at the policeman and gave a friendly smile; the collar under the knot of the gypsy's tie was open. It seemed to Bloch as if the gypsy was so deeply trapped that all he could do when he was touched on the arm was look at the policemen with helpless friendliness.

Bloch followed them into the building, which also housed the post office; for just a moment he believed that if anybody saw him eating a bread roll out in public, they could not possibly think that he was involved in anything. "Involved"? He could not even let himself think that he had to justify his presence here while they were bringing in the gypsy, by any action such as, say, eating bread rolls. He could justify himself only when he was questioned and accused of something; and because he had to avoid even thinking that he might be questioned, he also could not let himself think about how to prepare justifications in advance for this possibility – this possibility did not even exist. So if he was asked whether he had watched while the gypsy was being brought in, he would not have to deny it and pretend that he had been distracted because he was eating a bread roll but could admit that he had witnessed the event. "Witnessed"? Bloch interrupted himself while he waited in the post office for his phone call to be put through; "admit"? What did these words have to do with this event, which for him was of no significance. Didn't they give it a significance he was making every effort to deny? "Deny"? Bloch interrupted himself again. He had to keep his guard up against words that transformed what he wanted to say into some kind of statement.

His phone call was put through. Absorbed in avoiding the impression that he was prepared to make a statement, he caught himself wrapping a handkerchief over the receiver. Slightly disconcerted, he put the handkerchief back in his pocket. How had he come from the thought of unguarded talk to the handkerchief? He was told that the friend he was calling had to stay quartered with his team in a training camp until the important match on Sunday and could not be reached by phone. Bloch gave the postmistress another number. She asked him to pay for the first call first. Bloch paid and sat on a bench to wait for the second call. The phone rang and he stood up. But it was only a birthday telegram arriving. The post-

65

mistress wrote it down and confirmed it word by word. Bloch walked up and down. One of the postmen had returned from his round and was now loudly going over the details with the postmistress. Bloch sat down. Outside on the road, now that it was early afternoon, there was no distraction. Bloch had become impatient but did not show it. He heard the postman say that the gypsy had been hiding all this time near the border in one of the dugouts used by the customs men. "Anyone can say that," said Bloch. The postman turned towards him and stopped talking. What he claimed to be the latest news, Bloch went on, anybody could have read yesterday, the day before yesterday, even the day before the day before yesterday, in the papers. What he said didn't mean anything, nothing at all, nothing whatsoever. The postman had turned his back on Bloch even while Bloch was still talking and was now speaking quietly to the postmistress, in a murmur that sounded to Bloch like those passages in foreign films that are left untranslated because they are supposed to be incomprehensible anyway. He wasn't getting through to them any more. All at once the fact that it was in a post office that he "wasn't getting through any more" seemed to him not like a fact at all but like a bad joke, like one of those plays on words by, say, sportswriters, which he had always loathed. Even the postman's story about the gypsy had seemed to him crudely suggestive, a clumsy insinuation, like the birthday telegram, whose words were so commonplace that they simply could not mean what they said. And it wasn't only the conversation that was insinuating; everything around him was also meant to suggest something to him. "As though they were winking and making signs at me," thought Bloch. For what was it supposed to mean that the lid of the inkwell lay right next to it on the blotting paper and that the blotting paper on the desk had obviously been replaced just today, so that only a few impressions were legible on it? And wouldn't it be more proper to say "in order that" instead of "so that"? *In order that* the impressions would therefore be legible. And now the postmistress picked up the phone and

66

spelled out the birthday telegram letter by letter. What was she hinting at? What was behind her dictating "All the best," "With kind regards": what was that supposed to mean? Who was behind the cover name "your loving grandparents"? Even that morning in the paper, Bloch had instantly recognized the little advertisement which said "Why not phone?" as a trap.

It seemed to him as if the postman and the postmistress were in the know. "The postmistress and the postman," he corrected himself. Now the loathsome word-game sickness had struck even him, and in broad day light. "Broad day-light"? He must have hit on that phrase somehow. That expression seemed witty to him, in an unpleasant way. But were the other words in the sentence any better? If you said the word "sickness' to yourself, after a few repetitions you couldn't help laughing at it. "A sickness strikes me": silly. "I am stricken by a sickness": just as silly. "The postmistress and the postman"; "the postman and the postmistress"; "the post mistress and the postman": one big joke. Have you heard the one about the postman and the postmistress? "Everything seems like an inscription," thought Bloch: "THE BIRTH-DAY TELEGRAM," "THE INKWELL LID," "THE SCRAPS OF BLOTTING PAPER ON THE FLOOR." The rack where the various rubber stamps hung looked as if it had been sketched. He looked at it for a long time but could not work out what was supposed to be funny about the stand. On the other hand, there had to be a joke in it: otherwise, why should it look sketched to him? Or was it another trap? Was the thing there so that he would make a slip of the tongue? Bloch looked somewhere else, looked at another place, and looked somewhere else again. Does this ink pad mean anything to you? What do you think of when you see this completed cheque? What do you associate with that drawer's being open? It seemed to Bloch that he should take an inventory of the room, so that the objects he paused at or that he left out during his count could serve as evidence. The postman slapped the flat of his hand against the big bag that was still hanging from his shoulder. "The postman slaps the bag and takes it off," thought Bloch, word for word. "Now he puts it on the table and walks into the parcels room." He described the events to himself like a radio announcer to the public, as if this was the only way he could see them for himself. After a while it helped.

He stood still because the phone rang. As always when the phone rang, he felt he had known it would a moment before it did. The postmistress picked up the phone, then pointed to the phone box. Already inside the box, he asked himself whether perhaps he had misunderstood her gesture, if perhaps it had been meant for no one in particular. He picked up the receiver and asked his ex-wife, who had answered the phone with her first name only, as though she knew it was him, to send him some money poste restante. A peculiar silence followed. Bloch heard some whispering that wasn't meant for him. "Where are you?" the woman asked. He'd got cold feet and now he was high and dry, Bloch said and laughed as though he had said something extremely witty. The woman didn't answer. Bloch heard more whispering. It was very difficult said the woman. Why? asked Bloch. She hadn't been talking to him, answered the woman. "Where should I send the money?" His pockets would be empty soon if she didn't give him a hand, Bloch said. The woman kept quiet. Then the phone was hung up at her end.

"The snows of yesteryear," Bloch thought, unexpectedly, as he came out of the booth. What was that supposed to mean? In fact, he had heard that the undergrowth was so tangled and thick at the border that patches of snow could be found at certain spots even during the early summer. But that was not what he had meant. Besides, people had no business in the undergrowth. "No business"? How did he mean that? "The way I said it," thought Bloch.

At the savings bank he exchanged the American dollar bill he had carried with him for a long time. He also tried to exchange a Brazilian note, but the bank did not purchase that currency; besides, they didn't know the exchange rate.

When Bloch came in, the bank clerk was counting out coins, wrapping them up in rolls, and stretching rubber bands around the rolls. Bloch put the dollar bill on the counter. Next to it there was a music box; only when he gave it a second look did Bloch realize it was a contribution box for some charity. The clerk looked up but went on counting. Before he had been asked to, Bloch slid the note under the partition through to the other side. The clerk was lining up the rolls in a single row next to him. Bloch bent down and blew the note in front of the clerk, and the clerk unfolded the bill, smoothed it with the edge of his hand, and ran his fingertips over it. Bloch saw that his fingertips were quite black. Another clerk came out of the back room; to witness something, thought Bloch. He asked to have the exchange money – in which there was not even one note – put in an envelope and pushed the coins back under the partition. The official, in the same way he had lined up the piles earlier, stuffed the coins into an envelope and pushed the envelope back to Bloch. Bloch thought that if everybody asked to have their money put in envelopes, the savings bank would eventually go broke. You could do the same thing with everything you bought: maybe the heavy demand for packaging would slowly but surely drive businesses bankrupt? Anyway, it was fun to think about.

In a stationer's Bloch bought a tourist map of the region and had it well wrapped. He also bought a pencil; the pencil he asked to have put in a paper bag. With the rolled-up map in his hand, he walked on; he felt more harmless now than before, when his hands had been empty.

Outside the village, at a spot where he had a full view of the surrounding countryside, he sat down on a bench and, using the pencil, compared the details on the map with the items in the landscape in front of him. Key to the symbols: these circles meant a deciduous forest, those triangles a coniferous one, and when you looked up from the map, you were astonished that it was true. Over there, the terrain had to be swampy;

69

over there, there had to be a wayside shrine; over there, there had to be a level crossing. If you walked along this main road, you had to cross a bridge here, then had to come across a farm track, then had to walk up a steep incline, where, since somebody might be waiting at the top, you had to turn off the track and run across a field, had to run toward this forest – luckily, a coniferous forest – but someone might possible come at you out of the forest, so that you had to double back and then run down this slope toward this farmhouse, had to run past this shed, then run along this brook, had to leap over it at this spot because a jeep might come at you here, then zigzag across this field, slip through this hedge onto the road where a lorry was just going by, which you could stop and then you were safe. Bloch stopped short. "If it's a question of murder, your mind jumps from one thing to another," he had heard somebody say in a film.

He was relieved to discover a square on the map that he could not find in the landscape: the house that had to be there wasn't there, and the road that curved at this spot was in reality straight. It seemed to Bloch that this discrepancy might be helpful to him.

He watched a dog running towards a man in a field; then he realized that he was not watching the dog any more but the man, who was moving like somebody trying to block somebody else's way. Now he saw a little boy standing behind the man, and he realized that he was not watching the man and the dog, as would have been expected, but the boy, who, from this distance, seemed to be fidgeting; but then he realized that it was the boy's screaming that seemed like fidgeting to him. In the meantime, the man had grabbed the dog by the collar and all three, dog, man, and boy, had walked off in the same direction. "Who was that meant for?" thought Bloch.

On the ground in front of him a different picture: ants approaching a crumb of bread. He realized once again that he wasn't watching the ants but, on the contrary, the fly sitting on the bread crumb.

Everything he saw was conspicuous. The pictures did not seem natural but looked as if they had been made specifically for the occasion. They served some purpose. As you looked at them, they jumped out at you. "Like call-signs," thought Bloch. Like commands. When he closed his eyes and looked again afterwards, everything seemed to be different. The segments that could be seen seemed to glimmer and tremble at their edges.

From a sitting position, Bloch, without really getting up, had immediately walked away. After a while he stopped, then immediately broke into a run from a standing position. He got off to a quick start, suddenly stopped short, changed direction, ran at a steady pace, then changed his step, changed his step again, stopped short, then ran backwards, turned round while running backwards, ran forwards again, again turned round to run backwards, went backwards, turned round to run forwards, after a few steps changed to a sprint, stopped short, sat down on a kerb-stone, and immediately went back to running from a sitting position.

When he stopped and then walked on, the pictures seemed to dim from the edges inwards; finally they had turned completely black except for a circle in the middle. "As when somebody in a film looks through a telescope," he thought. He wiped the sweat off his legs with his trousers. He walked past a cellar where, because the cellar door was half open, tea leaves shimmered in a peculiar way. "Like potatoes," Bloch thought.

Of course the house in front of him had only one storey, the shutters were fastened, the roof tiles were covered with moss (another one of those words!), the door was closed, PRIMARY SCHOOL was written above it, in the garden somebody was chopping wood, it had to be the school caretaker, of course, and in front of the school naturally there was a hedge; yes, everything was in order, nothing was missing, not even the sponge underneath the blackboard in the gloomy classroom and the chalk box next to it, not even

71

the semicircles on the outside walls underneath the windows and the other marks that, by way of explanation, confirmed that these scratches were made by window hooks; in every respect it was as though everything you saw or heard confirmed to you that it was true to its word.

In the classroom the lid of the coal scuttle was open, and in the scuttle itself the handle of the coal shovel could be seen (an April fool's joke), and the floor with the wide boards, the cracks still wet from mopping, not forgetting the map on the wall, the sink next to the blackboard, and the corn cob husks on the windowsill; one single, cheap imitation. No, he would not let himself be tricked by April fool's jokes like these.

It was as if he were drawing wider and wider circles. He had forgotten the lightning conductor next to the door, and now it seemed to him like a cue. He was supposed to start. He helped himself out by walking around the school back to the yard and talking to the caretaker in the woodshed. Woodshed, caretaker, yard: cues. He watched while the caretaker put a log on the chopping block and lifted the axe. He said a couple of words from the yard; the caretaker stopped, answered, and as he hit the log, it fell to one side before he had struck it, and the axe hit the chopping block so that the pile of unchopped logs in the background collapsed. Another one of those cues. But the only thing that happened was that he called to the caretaker in the dim woodshed, asking whether this was the only classroom for the whole school, and the caretaker answered that for the whole school there was only this classroom.

No wonder the children hadn't even learned to read by the time they left school, the caretaker said suddenly, slamming the axe into the chopping block and coming out of the shed: they couldn't manage even to finish a single sentence of their own, they talked to each other almost entirely in single words, and they wouldn't talk at all unless you asked them to, and what they learned was only memorized stuff that they rattled off by rote; except for that, they couldn't use whole sentences. "Actually, all of them, more or less, have a speech

72

defect," said the caretaker.

What was that supposed to mean? What reason did the caretaker have for that? What did it have to do with him? Nothing? Yes, but why did the caretaker act as if it did have something to do with him?

Bloch should have answered, but he did not let himself get involved. Once he got started, he would have to go on talking. So he walked round the yard a while longer, helped the caretaker pick up the logs that had been flung out of the shed during the chopping, and then, little by little, wandered unobtrusively back out onto the road and was able to make his getaway with no trouble.

He walked past the playing field. It was after work, and the football team was practising. The ground was so wet that drops sprayed out from the grass when a player kicked the ball. Bloch watched for a while, but it was getting dark, and he left.

In the station buffet he had a snack and drank a couple of glasses of beer. On the platform outside, he sat on a bench. A girl in stiletto heels walked up and down on the gravel. A phone rang in the station master's office. One of the station staff stood in the door, smoking. Somebody came out of the waiting room and stopped again immediately. There was more rattling in the office, and loud talking, like somebody talking into a telephone, could be heard. It had grown dark by now.

It was fairly quiet. Here and there someone could be seen smoking a cigarette. A tap was turned on sharply and was turned off again at once – as though somebody had been startled. Farther away people were talking in the dark; faint sounds could be heard, as in a half-sleep: ah, ee. Somebody shouted: "Ow!" There was no way to tell whether a man or a woman had shouted. Very far away someone could be heard saying, very distinctly, "You look worn out." Between the railway lines, just as distinctly, a railway worker could be seen standing and scratching his head. Bloch thought he was

73

asleep.

An incoming train could be seen. You could watch a few passengers getting off, looking as if they were unsure about whether to get off or not. A drunk got off last of all and slammed the door shut. The railwayman on the platform could be seen as he gave a signal with his lamp, and then the train was leaving.

In the waiting room Bloch looked at the timetable. No more trains stopped at the station today. Anyway, it was late enough now to go to the cinema.

Some people were already sitting down in the foyer of the cinema. Bloch sat with them, his ticket in his hand. More and more people came. It was pleasant to hear so many sounds. Bloch went out in front of the cinema, stood out there with some other people, then went back inside.

In the film somebody shot a rifle at a man who was sitting far away at a campfire with his back turned. Nothing happened; the man did not fall over, just sat there, did not even look to see who had fired. Some time passed. Then the man slowly sank to one side and lay there without moving. That's the trouble with these old guns, the gunman said to his partner: no impact. But the man had actually been dead all the time he sat there at the campfire.

After the film Bloch rode out to the border with two men in a car. A stone banged against the bottom of the car. Bloch, who was in the back seat, became alert again.

Since this had been pay day, he could not find a table to himself at the pub. He sat down with some other people. The landlady came and put her hand on his shoulder. He understood and ordered drinks for the whole table.

To pay, he put a folded note on the table. Somebody next to him unfolded the note and said that another one might be tucked inside it. Bloch said, "So what?" and folded the note up again. The man unfolded the note again and pushed an ashtray on top of it. Bloch reached into the ashtray and threw the butts into the man's face. Somebody pulled his chair out from

74

under him, so that he slid under the table.

Bloch jumped up and in a moment had hit the man who had pulled away his chair hard in the chest with his forearm. The man fell against the wall and groaned loudly because he couldn't catch his breath. A couple of men twisted Bloch's arms behind his back and shoved him out through the door. He did not fall, just staggered a bit and ran right back in.

He swung at the man who had unfolded the note. He was kicked from behind, and he fell against the table with the man. Even while they were falling, Bloch was punching away at him.

Somebody grabbed him by the legs and hauled him away. Bloch kicked him in the ribs, and he let go. A few others got hold of Bloch and dragged him out. On the road they put a headlock on him and marched him around like that. They stopped in front of the customs shed with him, pushed his head against the doorbell, and went away.

A guard came out, saw Bloch standing there, and went back inside. Bloch ran after the men and tackled one of them from behind. The others rushed him. Bloch stepped to one side and butted his head into somebody's stomach. A few more people came out from the pub. Somebody threw a coat over his head. He kicked him in the shins, but somebody else was tying the arms of the coat together. Then they swiftly knocked him down and went back into the pub.

Bloch got loose from the coat and ran after them. One of them stopped but did not turn round. Bloch charged him; the man promptly moved off, and Bloch went sprawling on the ground.

After a while he got up and went into the pub. He wanted to say something, but when he moved his tongue, the blood in his mouth bubbled. He sat down at one of the tables and pointed with his finger to show that he wanted a drink. The barmaid brought him a bottle of beer without the glass. He thought he saw tiny flies running up and down the table, but it was just cigarette smoke.

He was too weak to lift the beer bottle with one hand; so he clutched it with both hands and bent over so that it didn't have to be lifted too high. His ears were so sensitive that at times the cards didn't drop onto the table but were slammed down, and at the bar the sponge didn't drop into the sink but slapped into it; and the landlady's daughter, with clogs on her bare feet, didn't walk through the bar but clattered through the bar; the wine didn't flow but gurgled into the glasses; and the music didn't play but boomed from the juke box.

He heard a woman scream in fright, but in a pub a woman's scream didn't mean anything; therefore, the woman could not have screamed in fright. Nevertheless, he had been jolted by the scream; it was only because of the noise, because the scream had been so shrill.

Little by little the other details lost their significance: the foam in the empty beer bottle meant no more to him than the cigarette box that the man next to him tore open just enough so that he managed to extract a single cigarette with his fingernails. Nor did the used matches lying loose everywhere in the cracks between the floorboards occupy his attention any more, and the fingernail impressions in the putty along the windowframe no longer seemed to have anything to do with him. Everything left him cold now, stood once more in its place; like peacetime, thought Bloch. The stuffed grouse above the juke box no longer forced one to draw conclusions; and the flies sleeping on the ceiling did not suggest anything any more.

You could see a man combing his hair with his fingers, you could see girls moving backwards as they danced, you could see men standing up and buttoning their coats, you could hear the noise the cards made as they were shuffled, but you didn't have to dwell on it any more.

Bloch got tired. The tireder he got, the more clearly he took everything in, distinguished one thing from another. He saw how the door invariably stayed open when somebody went out, and how somebody else always got up and shut it again.

76

He was so tired that he saw each thing by itself, especially the outline, as though there was nothing to the things but their outline. He saw and heard everything with total immediacy, without first having to translate it into words, as before, or comprehending it only in terms of words or word games. He was in a state where everything seemed natural to him.

Later the landlady sat down with him, and he put his arm around her so naturally that she did not even seem to notice. He dropped a couple of coins into the juke box as though it were nothing and danced effortlessly with the landlady. He noticed that every time she said something she added his name to it.

It wasn't important any more that he could see the barmaid clasping one hand in the other, nor was there anything special about the thick curtains, and it was only natural that more and more people left. They could be heard as they relieved themselves out on the street and then walked away.

It got quieter in the bar, so that the records in the juke box played very distinctly. In the pause between records people talked more softly or almost held their breath; it was a relief when the next record came on. It seemed to Bloch that you could talk about these occurrences as things that recurred forever; the course of a single day, he thought; things that you wrote about on picture postcards. "At night we sit in the pub and listen to records." He got tireder and tireder, and outside the apples were dropping off the trees.

When nobody but him was left, the landlady went into the kitchen. Bloch sat where he was and waited until the record was over. He turned off the juke box, so that now only the kitchen light was still on. The landlady sat at the table and did her accounts. Bloch approached her, a beer-mat in his hand. She looked up when he came out of the bar and looked at him as he approached her. He remembered the beer-mat too late; he wanted to hide it quickly, before she saw it, but the landlady looked away from him and at the beer-mat in his hand and asked him what he was doing with it, if perhaps she had

77

written a bill on it that hadn't been paid. Bloch dropped the beer-mat and sat down next to the landlady, not doing one thing smoothly after the other but hesitating at each move. She went on counting, talking to him at the same time, then cleared away the money. Bloch said he'd forgotten about the beer-mat in his hand, it hadn't meant anything.

She asked him to have something to eat with her. She set a wooden board in front of him. There was no knife, he said, though she had set the knife next to the board. She had to bring the washing in from the garden, she said, it was just starting to rain. It wasn't raining, he corrected her, it was only dripping from the trees because there was a little wind. But she had gone out already, and since she left the door open, he could see that it actually was raining. He saw her come back and shouted that she had dropped a shirt, but it turned out that it was only a rag for the floor, which had been lying near the doorway all along. When she lit the candle on the table, he saw the wax dripping onto a plate because she had tilted the candle slightly in her hand. She should watch out, he said, wax was dripping onto the clean plate. But she was already setting the candle in the spilled wax, which was still liquid, and pressing it down until it stood by itself. "I didn't know that you wanted to put the candle on the plate," Bloch said. She started to sit down where there was no chair, and Bloch shouted, "Watch out!" though she had just squatted to pick up a coin that had fallen under the table while she was counting. When she went into the bedroom, he immediately asked if she was all right, but she had only gone to see to the little girl; once when she left the table he even called after her to ask where she was going.

She turned on the radio on the kitchen-dresser; it was nice to watch her just walking about while music came out of the radio. When somebody in a film turned on the radio the pro- gramme was instantly interrupted for a bulletin about a wanted man.

As they sat at the table, they talked to each other. It seemed

78

to Bloch that he could not say anything serious. He cracked jokes, but the landlady took everything he said literally. He said that her blouse was striped like a football jersey and wanted to go on, but she asked him if he didn't like her blouse, what bothered him about it. It did no good to assure her that he had only made a joke and that the blouse went very nicely with her pale skin; she went on to ask if her skin was too pale for him. He said, jokingly, that the kitchen was furnished almost like a city kitchen, and she asked why he said "almost". Did people there keep their things cleaner? Even when Bloch made a joke about the estate owner's son (he'd proposed to her, hadn't he?) she took him literally and said the estate owner's son wasn't available. He tried to explain, using a comparison, that he had not meant it seriously, but she took the comparison literally as well. "I didn't mean to imply anything," Bloch said. "You must have had a reason for saying it," the landlady answered. Bloch laughed. The landlady asked why he was laughing at her.

The little girl called out from the bedroom. The landlady went in and calmed her down. When she came back, Bloch had stood up. She stood in front of him and looked at him for a while. But then she talked about herself. Because she was standing so close to him, he could not answer and took a step backward. She did not move after him, but hesitated. Bloch wanted to touch her. When he finally moved his hand, she looked to one side. Bloch let his hand drop and pretended that he had made a joke. The landlady sat down on the other side of the table and went on talking.

He wanted to say something, but then he could not think of what it was he wanted to say. He tried to remember: he could not remember what it was about, but it had something to do with disgust. Then a movement of the landlady's hand reminded him of something else. He could not think of what it was this time either, but it had something to do with shame. His perceptions of movements and things did not remind him of other movements and things but of sensations and feelings,

79

and he did not remember the feelings as if they were from the past but relived them as happening in the present: he did not remember shame and nausea but only felt ashamed and nauseated now that he remembered without being able to think of the things that had brought on the shame and nausea. The mixture of nausea and shame was so strong that his whole body started to itch.

A piece of metal knocked against the windowpane outside. The landlady answered his question by saying that it was the wire from the lightning conductor that had come loose. Bloch, who had seen a lightning conductor at the school, immediately concluded that this repetition was intentional; it could be no accident that he came across a lightning conductor twice in quick succession. Altogether he found everything alike; every object reminded him of every other object. What was the meaning of the repeated occurrence of lightning conductors? How should he interpret the lightning conductor? "Lightning conductor"? Surely that was just another play on words? Did it mean that he was safe from harm? Or did it indicate that he should tell the landlady everything? And why were the biscuits on the wooden plate fish-shaped? What did they suggest? Should he be "silent as a fish"? Was he not allowed to say any more? Was that what the biscuits on the wooden plate were trying to tell him? It was as if he did not see any of this but read it off a list of regulations on a notice-board.

Yes, they were regulations. The dish-cloth hanging over the tap was ordering him to do something. Even the cap of the beer-bottle left on the table, which had by now been cleared, demanded that he do something. Everything fell into place: everywhere he saw demands; to do one thing, not to do another. Everything was spelled out for him, the shelf where the spice boxes were, a shelf with jars of freshly made jam . . . things repeated themselves. Bloch noticed that for quite a while he had stopped talking to himself: the landlady was at the sink collecting bits of bread up out of the saucers. You had to clean up after him all the time, she said, he didn't even shut the table drawer when he took out the cutlery; books he had been looking through were just left open, he took off his coat and just let it drop where it was.

Bloch answered that he really felt that he would let everything drop. It wouldn't take much for him to let go of this ashtray in his hand, it even surprised him to see that the ashtray was still in his hand. He had stood up, still holding the ashtray in front of him. The landlady looked at him. He stared at the ashtray a while, then he put it down. As if in anticipation of the insinuations all around him, which repeated themselves, Bloch repeated it once more. He saw the landlady shake her arm over the sink. She said that a piece of apple had slipped up her sleeve and now it didn't want to come out. Didn't want to come out? Bloch imitated her by shaking his own sleeve. It seemed to him that if he imitated everything, he would stay on the safe side, so to speak. But she noticed it immediately and mimicked his imitation of her.

As she did that, she came close to the refrigerator, which had a cake box on top of it. Bloch watched her as she, still mimicking him, knocked the cake box from behind. Since he was watching her so intently, she threw her elbow back once more. The box began to slip and slowly tipped over the rounded edges of the refrigerator. Bloch could still have caught it, but he watched until it hit the floor.

While the landlady bent down to pick up the box, he walked up and down; wherever he stopped he pushed things away from him into a corner – a chair, a lighter on the stove, an egg cup on the kitchen table. "Is everything all right?" he asked. He asked her what he wanted her to ask him. But before she could answer, something knocked on the window in a way a wire from a lightning conductor would never knock against a pane. Bloch had known it a moment beforehand.

The landlady opened the window. A customs guard was outside asking to borrow an umbrella for the walk back to town. Bloch said that he might as well go along with him, and the landlady handed him the umbrella which hung under the overalls on the doorframe. He promised to bring it back the next day. As long as he hadn't brought it back, nothing could go wrong.

Out on the road he opened the umbrella; the rain was coming down so hard that he did not hear whether she had answered him. The guard came running along the wall of the house to get under the umbrella, and they started off.

They were only a few steps away when the light in the pub was turned off and it became completely dark. It was so dark that Bloch put his hand over his eyes. Behind the wall that they were just passing he heard the snorting of cows. Something ran past him. "I almost stepped on a hedgehog just then!" the guard exclaimed.

Bloch asked how he could have seen a hedgehog in the dark. The guard answered, "That's part of my profession. Even if all you see is one movement or hear just one noise, you must be able to identify the thing that made that movement or sound. Even when something moves at the very edge of your vision, you must be able to recognize it, in fact even be able to determine what colour it is, though actually you can recognize colours only at the centre of the retina." They had passed the houses by the border by now and were walking along a short-cut beside the brook. The path was covered with sand of some kind, which became lighter as Bloch grew more accustomed to the dark.

"Of course, we're not kept very busy here," the guard said. "Since the border was mined, there's been no smuggling going on here any more. So your alertness slips, you get tired and can't concentrate any more. And then when something does happen, you don't even react."

Bloch saw something running towards him and stepped behind the guard. A dog brushed past him as it ran past.

"And then if somebody suddenly steps in front of you, you don't even know how you should grab hold of him. You're in the wrong position from the start and when you finally get yourself right, you depend on your partner, who is standing

82

next to you, to catch him, and all along your partner is depending on you to catch him yourself – and the man you're after gives you the slip." The slip? Bloch heard the customs guard next to him under the umbrella take a deep breath.

Behind him the sand crunched. He turned around and saw that the dog had come back. They walked on, the dog running alongside sniffing at the backs of his knees. Bloch stopped, broke off a hazelnut twig by the brook, and chased the dog away.

"If you're facing each other," the guard went on, "it's important to look the other man in the eyes. Before he starts to run, his eyes show which direction he'll take. But you've also got to watch his legs at the same time. Which leg is he putting his weight on? The direction that leg is pointing is the direction he'll want to take. But if he wants to fool you and not run in that direction, he'll have to shift his weight just before he takes off, and that takes so much time that you can rush him in the meantime."

Bloch looked down at the brook, whose roaring could be heard but not seen. A heavy bird flew up out of a thicket. Chickens in a coop could be heard scratching and pecking their beaks against the wooden wall.

"Actually, there aren't any hard-and-fast rules," said the guard. "You're always at a disadvantage because the other man also watches to see how you're reacting to him. All you can ever do is react. And when he starts to run, he'll change his direction after the first step and you're the one whose weight is on the wrong foot."

Meanwhile, they had got back onto the made up road and were approaching the edge of the village. They stepped on patches of wet sawdust which the rain had swept out on to the road. Bloch asked himself whether the reason the guard went into so much detail about something that could be said in one sentence was that he was really trying to say something else. "He spoke *from memory*," thought Bloch. As a test, he himself started to talk at great length about something that usually required only one sentence, but the guard seemed to think that this was completely natural and didn't ask him what he was driving at. So the guard seemed to have meant what he said before quite literally.

In the middle of the village some people who had been at a dancing class came toward them. "Dancing class"? What did that phrase suggest? One girl had been searching for something in the "handbag" as she passed, and another had been wearing boots with "high tops". Were these abbreviations for something? He heard the handbag snapping shut behind him; he almost folded up his umbrella in reply.

He held the umbrella over the customs guard as far as the council flats. "So far I'm only renting, but I'm saving up to buy," said the guard, standing in the stair-hall. Bloch had come in too. Would he like to come up for a drink? Bloch refused but stood still. The lights went off again while the guard was going up the stairs. Bloch leaned against the letter-boxes downstairs. Outside, quite high up, a plane flew past. "The mail plane," the guard shouted down into the dark, and pushed the light switch. It echoed in the stairwell. Bloch had quickly gone out.

At the hotel he learned that a large tourist group had arrived and had been put up on camp-beds in the bowling alley; that's why it was so quiet down there tonight. Bloch asked the girl who told him about this if she wanted to come upstairs with him. She answered, gravely, that that was impossible tonight. Later, in his room, he heard her walk down the hall and go past his door. The rain had made the room so cold that it seemed to him as if damp sawdust had been spread all over it. He put the umbrella tip-down in the wash-basin and lay on the bed fully dressed.

Bloch became sleepy. He made a few tired gestures to make light of his sleepiness, but that made him even sleepier. Various things he had said during the day came back to him; he tried to get rid of them by breathing out. Then he felt himself falling asleep; like before the end of a paragraph, he thought. Pheasants were flying through fire, and beaters were walking alongside a cornfield, and the porter was standing in the boxroom writing the room number in chalk on his briefcase, and a leafless thornbush was full of swallows and snails.

He woke up gradually and realized that somebody was breathing loudly in the next room and that the rhythm of the breathing was forming itself into sentences in his half-sleep; he heard the exhale as a long-drawn-out "and", and the extended sound of the inhale then transformed itself inside him into sentences that – after the dash that corresponded to the pause between the inhale and the exhale – invariably attached themselves to the "and". Soldiers with pointed civilian shoes were standing in front of the cinema, and the match-box was lying on the cigarette packet, and a vase was standing on the television, and a truck filled with sand covered the bus with dust as it went by, and a hitch-hiker was holding a bunch of grapes in his other hand, and outside the door somebody was saying, "Open up, please."

"Open up, please." Those last three words did not fit at all into the breathing from next door, which became more and more distinct while the sentences were slowly beginning to fade out. He was wide awake now. Somebody knocked on the door again and said, "Open up, please." He must have been woken by that, since the rain had stopped.

He sat up quickly, a bedspring snapped back into place, the chambermaid was outside the door with the breakfast tray. he hadn't ordered breakfast, he could barely manage to say, before she had excused herself and knocked on the door across the hall.

Alone in the room, he found everything re-arranged. He turned on the tap. A fly immediately fell off the mirror into the sink and was washed away at once. He sat down on the bed: just now that chair had been to his right, and now it was to his left. Was the picture reversed? He looked at it from left to right, then from right to left. He repeated the look from left to right; this look seemed to him like reading. He saw a "ward-robe", "then" "a" "waste-paper-basket", "then" "a" "curtain"; while looking from right to left, however, he saw⌐, next to it the ⊓⊓, under it the ◖, next to it the ▢▢, on top of it his ▱; and when he looked around, he saw the ▯, next to it the Ⓐ and the ⊙. He sat on the⌐—⌐, under it there was a ▬, next to it a ⊏⊐. He went to the ▦ : ⊞⊟ :

⛏ 🚲 ✉ 🍶 🧴 Bloch closed the curtains and went out.

The dining room downstairs was filled with the tourists. The proprietor led Bloch into the other room, where the proprietor's mother was sitting in front of the television with the curtains closed. The proprietor opened the curtains and stood next to Bloch; once Bloch saw him standing to his left; then, when he looked up again, it was the other way round. Bloch ordered breakfast and asked for the newspaper. The proprietor said that the tourists were reading it just at the moment. Bloch ran his fingers over his face; his cheeks seemed to be numb. He felt cold. The flies on the floor were crawling so slowly that at first he mistook them for beetles. A bee rose from the windowsill but fell back immediately. The people outside were leaping over the puddles; they were carrying heavy shopping bags. Bloch ran his fingers all over his face.

The proprietor came in with the tray and said that the news-paper still wasn't free. He spoke so softly that Bloch also spoke softly when he answered. "There's no hurry," he whispered. The television screen now looked dusty in the daylight, and the window that the schoolchildren looked through as they walked past was reflected in it. Bloch ate and listened to the programme. The proprietor's mother moaned from time to time.

Outside he noticed a stand with a bag full of newspapers. He went outside, dropped a coin into the slot next to the bag, and then took out a paper. He had so much practice in opening papers that he read the description of himself even as he was going inside. He had attracted a woman's attention on the bus because some change had fallen out of his pocket; she had bent down for it, and had noticed that it was American money. Subsequently, she had heard that similar coins had been found beside the dead cashier. No one took her story seriously at first, but then it turned out that her description matched the description given by one of the cashier's boyfriends who, when he called for the cashier in his car the night before the murder, had seen a man standing near the cinema.

Bloch sat down again in the other room and looked at the picture they had drawn of him according to the woman's description. Did that mean that they did not know his name yet? When had the paper been printed? He saw that it was the first edition, which usually came out the evening before. The headline and the picture looked to him as if they had been pasted onto the paper; like newspapers in films, he thought, where they replace the real headlines with headlines that fit the film; or like those headlines you could have made up about yourself in amusement arcades.

The doodles in the margin had been deciphered as the word "Stumm" and, moreover, with a capital at the beginning; so it was probably a proper name. Was a person named Stumm involved in the matter? Bloch remembered telling the cashier about his friend Stumm, the football player.

When the girl cleared the table, Bloch did not close the paper. He learned that the gypsy had been released, that the mute schoolboy's death had been an accident. The paper carried only a school picture of the boy because he had never been photographed alone.

A cushion that the proprietor's mother was using as a back-rest fell from the armchair onto the floor. Bloch picked it up and went out with the paper. He saw the hotel's copy lying on the card-table; the tourists had left by now. The paper – it was the weekend edition – was so thick that it did not fit into the rack.

When a car drove past him, he stupidly – for it was quite bright out – wondered why its headlights were turned off. Nothing in particular happened. He saw the boxes of apples being poured into sacks in the orchards. A bicycle that passed him skidded a bit in the mud. He saw two farmers shaking hands in the doorway of a shop; their hands were so dry that he could hear them chafing against each other. Muddy tractor marks led out from the farm tracks onto the asphalt of the road. He saw an old woman bent over in front of a shop window, a finger to her lips. The parking spaces in front of the shops were emptying; the customers who were still arriving went in through the back door. "Suds" "poured" "over" "the doorsteps". "Featherbeds" "were lying" "behind" "the" "windowpanes". The blackboards listing prices were carried back into the shops. "The chickens" "pecked at" "grapes that had been dropped." The turkeys squatted heavily in the wire cages in the orchards. The girl assistants stood outside the shop-door and put their hands on their hips. The owner stood inside the dark shop, absolutely still behind his scales. "Lumps of yeast" "lay" "on the counter". Bloch stood against the wall of a house. There was an odd sound when a casement window that was ajar next to him opened all the way. He had walked on immediately.

He stopped in front of a brand-new building that was still unoccupied but already had glass in its windows. The rooms were so empty that the countryside behind the house could be seen through the windows. Bloch felt as though he had built the house himself. He himself had installed the electric sockets and even glazed the windows. The crowbar, the sandwich papers, and the plastic food container had also been left on the windowsill by him.

He took a second look: no, the light switches remained light switches, and the garden chairs behind the house remained garden chairs.

He walked on because –

Did he have to give a reason for walking, so that – ?

What did he have in mind when – ? Did he have to justify the "when" by – ? Did this go on until – ? Had he reached the point where – ?

Why did anything have to be inferred from the fact that he was walking here? Did he have to give a reason for stopping here? Why did he have to have something in mind when he walked past a swimming pool?

These "so thats", "becauses", and "whens" were like regulations; he decided to avoid them in order not to –

It was as if a window that was slightly ajar was quietly opened beside him. Everything thinkable, everything visible, was occupied. It was not a scream that startled him but a sentence upside down on the top of a series of normal sentences. Everything seemed to have been newly named.

The shops were already closed. The window displays, now that nobody was walking up and down in front of them any more, looked too full. Not a single spot was without at least a pile of tinned foods on it. A half-torn receipt hung out of the cash register. The shops were so tidied up that . . .

"The shops were so tidied up that you couldn't point to anything any more because . . ." "The shops were so tidied up that you couldn't point to anything any more because the individual items hid each other." The parking spaces were now completely empty except for the shop girls' bicycles.

After lunch Bloch went to the playing field. Even from far away he heard the spectators' screaming. When he got there, the reserves were still playing a pre-game match. He sat on a bench at the side of the pitch and read the paper as far as the supplements. He heard a sound as if a chunk of meat had

89

fallen on a stone floor; he looked up and saw that the wet heavy ball had smacked off a player's head.

He got up and walked away. When he came back, the main match had already started. The benches were filled, and he walked alongside the pitch to the space behind the goal. He did not want to stand too close behind the goal, and he climbed up the bank to the road. He walked along the road as far as the corner flag. It seemed to him that a button was coming off his jacket and bouncing on the road; he picked up the button and put it in his pocket.

He started talking to some man who was standing next to him. He asked which teams were playing and about their place in the league. They shouldn't play the ball so high in a strong wind like this, he said.

He noticed that the man next to him had buckles on his shoes. "I don't know either," the man answered. "I'm a salesman, and I'm here for only a few days."

"The men are shouting much too much," Bloch said. "A good game goes very quietly."

"There's no coach to tell them what to do from the sidelines," answered the man. It seemed to Bloch as though they were talking to each other for the benefit of some third party.

"On a small field like this you have to decide very quickly when to pass," he said.

He heard a slap as if the ball had hit a goalpost. Bloch spoke about how he had once played against a team whose players were all barefoot; every time they kicked the ball, the slapping sound had gone right through him.

"In the stadium I once saw a player break his leg," the salesman said. "You could hear the crack at the back of the terraces."

Bloch saw the other spectators around him talking to each other. He did not watch the one who happened to be speaking but always watched the one who was listening. He asked the salesman whether he had ever tried to look away from the forwards at the beginning of an offensive and, instead, to look at

90

the keeper whose goal the forwards were approaching.

"It's very difficult to take your eyes off the forwards and the ball and watch the goalie," Bloch said. "You have to tear yourself away from the ball; it's a completely unnatural thing to do." Instead of seeing the ball, you saw how the goalkeeper, his hands on his thighs, running forward, retreating, back and forth swerving to the left and right and shouting to his defence. "Usually you don't notice him until the ball has been shot at the goal."

They walked along the sideline together. Bloch heard panting as though a linesman were running past them. "It's a strange sight to watch the goalie running back and forth like that, without the ball but expecting it," he said.

He couldn't watch that way for very long, answered the salesman; you couldn't help but look back at the forwards. If you looked at the goalkeeper, it seemed as if you had to look cross-eyed. It was like seeing somebody walk toward the door and instead of looking at the man you looked at the doorknob. It made your head hurt, and you couldn't breathe properly any more.

"You get used to it," said Bloch, "but it's ridiculous."

A penalty kick was called. All the spectators rushed behind the goal.

"The goalkeeper is trying to work out which corner the man taking the kick will aim for," Bloch said. "If he knows the player, he knows which corner he usually goes for. But probably the man taking the penalty is also reckoning that the goalie has worked this out himself. So the goalie has to go on working out that just today the ball might go into the other corner. But what if the man taking the kick follows the goalkeeper's thinking and plans to shoot into the usual corner after all? And so on, and so on."

Bloch could see all the players gradually clearing the penalty area. The penalty kicker adjusted the ball. Then he too backed out of the penalty area.

"When the kicker starts his run, the goalkeeper

unconsciously shows with his body which way he'll throw himself even before the ball is kicked, and the kicker can simply kick in the other direction," Bloch said. "The goalie might just as well try prizing open a door with a piece of straw."

The kicker suddenly started his run. The goalkeeper, who was wearing a bright yellow jersey, stood absolutely still, and the penalty kicker shot the ball into his hands.